Harry the Flat is dead and buried in the backstretch of
Aqueduct Raceway. This is causing the Mob no end of
trouble on the betting side, so Harry's oldest and
dearest friend—now carrying on with Harry's widow,
Gertrude nee Hawkins, in Harry's absence, and in
debt to the Mob for $1500—is persuaded to dig him
up after the eighth race. Tony Winner, low level Mob
boss, is very specific on this point, and to that end has
had a time bomb surgically implanted in our hero's
thigh to impress upon him the urgency of this matter.

So on this fateful day, off he goes to the Aqueduct in
Queens, New York, with a cello case stuffed with a

pick and a shovel, prepared to dig up the
dubious remains of Harry the Flat so that the
Mob's control of horserace betting is no
longer compromised. His mind is filled with
thoughts of Harry, of Gertrude, of his ex-
wife, and all the schemes and plans and bets
that led to this moment. It will be a long day
for our hero. He has a lot to learn about
horse racing.

Underlay

by Barry N. Malzberg

STARK
HOUSE

Stark House Press • Eureka California

UNDERLAY

Published by Stark House Press
1315 H Street
Eureka, CA 95501, USA
griffinskye3@sbcglobal.net
www.starkhousepress.com

ISBN: 1-933586-85-0
ISBN-13: 978-1-933586-85-4

Text set in
Additional design and text layout by Mark Shepard, shepdesign.home.com-
cast.net
Proofreading by Rick Ollerman

First Stark House Press Edition: June 2015
FIRST EDITION

Underlay

By Barry N. Malzberg

For Joyce, Stephanie Jill
and
Erika Cornell Malzberg
and for
Fred Caposella

"We would of all by now been wearing diamonds;
But we ran out of money too soon."
Public Domain

CONTENTS

Underlay

I

MY MISSION AT AQUEDUCT RACETRACK
IN OZONE PARK, QUEENS, NEW YORK

My mission is to recover the body of the late but famous Harry the Flat and to present it, only incidentally, to his widow Gertrude, so that he may be given a respectable funeral. It is high time that this honor was paid him. He died four years ago of a cerebral accident and now lies encased in heat and ice, sweat and dust, death and connection, underneath the backstretch of this well-known race track which is one of the top sporting centers, it is widely understood, on absolutely the entire East Coast of the United States. Gertrude is most unhappy about the indignity of Harry's station, to say nothing of his many friends and acquaintances who did not abandon their friendship for Harry the Flat simply because he died and was thus unable to reimburse his debts. In addition to these emotional factors there is a practical difficulty: his continued presence under the backstretch has been lousing up the mob's figure, this being the prime reason for the recovery action.

Unfortunately, and as is usually the case in this fiction called life, there are complications. The NYRA, for one thing, which is short for the New York Racing Association, the governing authority of racing in this state under the aegis of the popular and successful Nelson A. Rockefeller, would not look kindly upon its backstretch at Aqueduct Racetrack, in deepest Queens, being dug up . . . nor does it appreciate the recreational facilities being used as an arena for anything other than the simpler human passions. Accordingly, as the one charged with this important mission, I must move cautiously and with a certain overriding sense of the dignity of my position.

There are several reasons for this sensation of great pressure which afflicts me, the most important of which is that the recovery must be made today, June 9, 1971, and not a moment later. Precisely at midnight tonight, the bomb which the mob has implanted within my thigh as the signature of their seriousness will explode and blow me out of reach of all saving parlays unless I have, sometime during the interim, presented the body of one Harry the Flat as ransom for being defused. The excellent George Needles, who is the mob specialist in occupational and internal therapy, will do the defusing if given the proper word. If anyone else so much as looks at this area in a compromising fashion the bomb will blow up. I am assured of this by Tony Winner, who has never lied to me about a thing in his life.

This would be an irrevocable disaster, the bomb going off inside me, I mean. I am really only forty-one years old recently, even younger than the great John Fitzgerald Kennedy was when he was assassinated and I retain an even greater enthusiasm than did this famous historical figure for, what I like to think of as, life.

II

A DESCRIPTION OF HARRY THE FLAT
AS I REMEMBER HIM. OF COURSE,
IT HAS BEEN A WHILE

He is a small man, crushed halfway between his hat and the ground, the white tremble of his features alight with occasional grins and nods, the strangely heavy lips pouting in a thin bow when he is verbally assaulted. His frequent talk is in an uneven slang composed of mid-Manhattan and outer Queens. Because he served in the Army, he is also capable of cursing with a fluent Southern bias, usually in anal inferences. When he walks he bounces, and so has cultivated a loser's trudge to conceal imminent fortune. He wears damp, sagging suits which seem to glisten with sweat and purposeful creases. His pockets are filled with papers of every description: tip-sheets, scorecards, computations, mathematical tables, pornographic playing cards and so on. He prefers Lawton's Orange Sheet but has been known to buy a Powell. He distrusts the *New York Turf Letter* but has been known to play its criss-cross double selections. He dislikes touts but will solicit strangers' views on forthcoming races. He appreciates longshots whose odds drop consistently to post and go off at less than eight to one.

He has been married for the seven years up to the point of his death to the lovely Gertrude nee Hawkins who comforts him, prepares his meals, and arranges occasional loans and grants to him. Every night, whether he wants it or not, she offers the precarious advantages of her large white body, endowed under stress, with an almost plastic mobility. He prefers Scotch but will drink beer. He prefers beer but will drink wine. He prefers wine but will drink rum. He will not abstain although he is concerned about his liver. Occasionally, he has gone through periods of abrupt withdrawal from alcohol, composed of gloom and an obsessive determination to urinate less. He believes that Johnny Ruane has never reached his true potential and that Eddie Belmonte is dishonest. He does not believe in wheeling to favorites on the daily doubles, particularly if the favorite in either race is less than eight to five. He sweats, eliminates, excretes, and performs other human tasks but has never been known to have regarded them as much other than horrid necessities. If he goes to the men's room with you it is silently understood that this is only because he is trying to be sociable.

III

WHY I HAVE BEEN SELECTED
FOR THIS MISSION

I was the oldest living friend of Harry the Flat when he was with us; now that he is gone he remains my closest dead friend. Furthermore, I am the only one who is sufficiently aware of the metaphysical, not to say philosophical, underlay of so many of his most famous opinions. Thus there is a good deal of sentiment wound into this. It is not an annoyance which I will be removing from the backstretch but a sacrament, meaning that I will take especial care of the decomposing layers of Harry the Flat as I cradle him across the infield lake and out into the parking lot. A less involved person might do work less neat, leaving various evidences for the law.

Also, and aside from all this sentiment, I am in dead hock to the mob, which has their own important reasons for wishing to remove his body. These reasons have nothing to do with salvaging the good will of the widow. The way in which they will aid my recovery is this: they are rigging the eighth race. In this race, Knockover, a one hundred and fifty to one shot, will win by four to five lengths breezing. Thereby, the mob feels, it will cause such astonishment and consternation in the grandstand, infield, clubhouse, and steward's offices that I will be able to stumble into the backstretch undetected and, spade and shovel in hand, do the disinterment, hurl the uncoffined corpse over my strong right shoulder and speed away. There is no possibility that Knockover will not win this race. I have been informed that it has been irrevocably manipulated for him, barring the omnipresent prospect of poor racing luck or blind switches. In which case, of course—well, in which case I will have to remove Harry anyway because the mob has selected today, June 9th, as the target date and there is no tomorrow for the efficient and well-functioning Mob.

(It cannot be done at night. The track is patrolled by thin and solemn guards, busted-out horse-players all, with guns for programs and clubs for Lawton; they will brook neither mystery nor possibility. Also, and I admit this, the Mob is perverse and has an almost literary sense of irony in certain details; they feel it is fitting that the decomposed Harry be removed in this time and in this way. Since the Mob itself need not be up front, this has the aspect of reasonable thinking, to them. I have no choice but to accept this.)

There is no tomorrow for the Mob; there was no tomorrow for the unfortunate and unforgettable Harry the Flat either.

Only the Mob itself can transcend time; coexisting at the poles, moving between eternity and origin like a dark fish in gelatin, the cool, spacious eaves of chronology firming its flesh as it strokes my life tenderly, absently, a dim caress moving me toward such intricate and deadly causation.

IV

A STILL LIFE OF HARRY THE FLAT ON
ONE OF THOSE RARE BUT STILL-
CELEBRATED OCCASIONS
WHEN HE WAS FUCKING
HIS WIFE

He hangs over her, mouth open, balancing on the palms, knees at cross-angle to the skylight, looking at the whiteness of the walls, the yellow background, that yawning pit of his wife which seems to smile at him as he guides himself gracelessly into that cavern, feeling it swaddle and surround him while he sucks on her breasts, biting the nipples absently while he computes results, balances, odds-charts—the only way in which he is able to force himself into a state sufficiently abstracted to function. It is four to five against coming fast. It is seven to two against her coming; even money, however, that if she comes at all she comes first. Make that a round-robin. It is twenty-three to one against simultaneous orgasm, well, make that nineteen to one instead. Nevertheless, even knowing all of this so well he persists; there is really very little alternative after all, the odds are fascinating and in any event there is nothing better to do at the present moment that he has not yet already done to avoid the situation. Caught in that hush, in that slow, clinging languor one can sense his trembling eyes as he looks with slow, cold astonishment toward the ceiling. The first drops of the parlay begin to build within him.

He surges toward her then, the heart of him caught in a trap larger and containing more torment than any... any which he has ever known before... any but for this reiterated snatch.

V

THE LAST SERMON OF HARRY THE
FLAT AS DELIVERED TO FRIENDS
AND ACQUAINTANCES ON THE
EVE OF HIS DEATH, JUNE 18,
1967, AT POP WARNER'S BAR
AND GRILL IN FLUSHING,
QUEENS, NEW YORK

"My friends, we are about to return, but not to a quality of vision. Rather, we seek a vision of quality. The spirit that I now reflect, moves slowly within us to disgorge its own insight. Pain, like a memory drifting through our skulls, in the words of the good poet Aeschlyus, moves past the body's core and toward its own destination.

"We have busted out flatly, once again... but I tell you this: that there has come upon this planet a newer generation of horseplayer, a horseplayer fired and forged in the testing and drone, droned and tested in the forge of the fire... and this generation will not easily sacrifice its margin, nor permit, for two bits, the denial of a program. It is not a generation which will submit cheaply to the lash of dime breakage, one which will accept the slavery and humiliation of an eighteen percent take out.

"No, I say to you my friends and brothers, no! To all of you, sharers of one destiny, I say that we have come to that time when the reversals will begin, a massive turning of the time, and friends and losers alike, parlaying our nine to one shots across the board, we will get out of the slime hole of history and move toward that greater achievement which once we dreamed was our contract when we got into this game. Why did we get into this game?

"I will answer that question: we came to this game not for a victory of personality but for a personality of victory. And I say to you now, letting the word flow forth, that there will be an end to losing favorites, worthless longshots, missed wheels, terrified and cowardly apprentices ruining our figures. The war is now turning around and in our favor. Daylight through the end of the tunnel. We will clean out the poison from all crevices that exist and then move on to other things.

"And so I say to you... I say that we will go into the streets now and toward our homes tonight, performing the old, cold, graceful motions which we have carried on so many times on the way to wipe out. But I tell you that this time, this night, is different and the motions are not an intimation of loss so much as a loss of intimation. On the other hand, they may be neither intimatory nor lustful but only a grave sensuality, that slow dance of the spirit. We cannot lose. And we will not lose. For we have seen the reign of the good and evil in our time: Marshall, Rainey, Cordero, Rotz, Jacobson, Fitzsimmons, Baeza, Smithwick, Shoemaker, P.J. Bailey, W. Lester, and we have survived. Our survival becomes mute witness to the century's terror.

"We turn toward the night knowing that the night will yet turn toward us. And now I bid you good evening. Good evening, gentlemen, and quiet to your homes: we shall assemble later and there will be a greatness among us."

VI

FURTHER EXPLANATION OF MY MOTIVES

I am enlisted to disentomb the body of the late and famous Harry the Flat because my own position with the Mob is precarious. Simply stated (I might as well come to the point) I owe out fifteen hundred dollars which fifteen hundred dollars I do not have and only because of being carried along by the good graces of Tony Winner for several months now have I avoided a rock in the head at any moment. Now is the time to function; I have been given this excellent chance to redeem myself, recoup my debts, and live a free life. If I can only perform this one service for the Mob, things will be good. I am dedicated to success. I know I will not fail.

I want to make the Mob happy. The alternative, after all, is too hard to contemplate. Not only have I put my life on the line as has been previously annotated, I have this enormous and very far-reaching sentiment for the late Harry the Flat to further my overall sense of dedication.

VII

HOW GERTRUDE NEE HAWKINS FELT
ABOUT HARRY THE FLAT

"He's a stiff. What I mean is he don't produce. If he produced, that would be one thing, but half the time he's straight down the drain. The other half he's telling me he's on the way up but I don't see no evidence of the fact. I don't see nothing but that he gets deeper and deeper which I can always tell from his eyes. Call me a pessimist but I have my opinions on this.

"I got to have my head examined or something like that just to string along with a guy like this one let alone be married. But there's something very lovable about him, okay, okay. Anyway, I got to admit that with him every day is a difference. Not that I was getting any younger, either. You never know what's going to happen next with him though except it'll be something bad, but nothing else, so there's all that anticipation which can be really terrific. The other way I know how I would've ended up. This way there are lots of questions. You follow?

"Besides that, Harry arranged for the sterilization right after the accident and everything. So that's out of the picture which is a relief knowing that nothing like that will ever happen again. I wouldn't bring children into this world, anyhow.

"Oh, it's not a bad life, not the worst life, when you look at it from the outside. From the inside is a little different thing, but I read somewhere where one of these guys wrote that everybody's life, from the inside, looks terrible. And there's a kind of security in it, too.

"But who would believe, would you ever believe, that there could be such pain in that place? Would you?"

VIII

THE TEXT OF A TIP SHEET WHICH HARRY
THE FLAT SENT OUT TO A LARGE
RANDOM MAILING OF PEOPLE
ONE WEEK WHEN HE WAS IN
DEEP AND UNABLE TO RAISE
MONEY FROM THE SHYLOCKS
WHO WERE GETTING A
SEVERE CASE OF THE
HARRY-THE-FLAT
SHORTS THAT
WINTER

"I must win or I'm out of business! I must win Tuesday, August 10, 1960, or never be heard from again. This is serious business. Do not destroy this notice. Read it carefully!

"Yes, on Tuesday, August 10, 1960, selected associates and I have elected to put over one of the great sporting COUPS of the New York racing season, a COUP in which investors will find a solid horse, well-placed, in clever hands and ready to win. This horse will go off as a SLEEPER at a guaranteed payment of twelve to one or more!

"This COUP has been in the planning for several months. My associates and I have worked carefully toward this day, using our avenues of connection to assure happiness for selected investors. Now at last the time has arrived. And you are invited to get aboard. Your name has been given me by a confidential source who I cannot mention who assures that your confidence may be respected and your sincere interest in horse-racing cannot be doubted.

"We ask you for no money!

"That is correct, we ask you for no money. My associates and I, we stand behind our predictions one hundred percent, without fear and without favor. If you wish to know the name of this horse you may do so at no fee whatsoever. Simply call us at the number given below between the hours of nine a.m. and twelve noon on Monday, August 9th, 1960.

"Your only obligation will be to forward us the proceeds of a five dollar win bet on this COUP *AFTER* the race has been run.

"In order to cover the modest expenses for this mailing and to obtain proof or your own serious interest in this once in a lifetime opportunity, we do request only that you give us a small deposit prior to our release of the name of the COUP horse.

"This deposit may be deducted from the eventual sum you will forward when the horse wins. If you will mail this deposit to the address shown below and sign the name of the person to whom you wish the information released, my associates and I will then accept your call on Monday, August 9th, and release to you the name of this horse.

"The deposit required is only fifteen dollars and since the horse must pay more than fifteen to one, you will see how reasonable this small statement of faith and cooperation is.

"This is serious business. We are not fooling! The horse must surely win because if it does not I am out of business. It is not my intention to play on your faith, time, small deposit, or risk unless I can produce for you. So I say once again, as I did before, that this horse will win at odds of no less than twelve to one or better.

"Send your deposit in immediately. If you have a friend who, you feel, might want to accompany you into the COUP, please pass this letter on to him. We must advise you, however, that we will accept only a limited number of investors, inasmuch as the odds must be kept as high as possible on the horse in order to guarantee a real PLUM to my associates, myself, and to those willing to join us in this fantastic day of fun and games at the track on COUP DAY.

"Remember, the deposit necessary is only fifteen dollars, the best investment of your life.

"Only fifteen dollars."

IX

HOW I GOT HERE

I got here in various and circuitous ways beginning with the difficult and always interesting moments of conception-and-birth but most specifically, which is a question of keeping things in direct context, I followed the turf advice of Harry the Flat.

I followed his turf advice in relation to the system number 34, which system involves playing platers or two year old claiming geldings in a modified-progression situation. I got took to a considerable extent, even though I was able, in the middle of all the troubles, to hit a ninety-six dollar and seventy cent payoff only to see it taken off the board because of a tiny little disqualification. This was frustrating but did not break the basic pattern which was disastrous.

I do not, however, blame Harry the Flat for what has happened to me, inasmuch as he prepared this system a long time ago in the Eisenhower era. So he is unaware of the more current realities of racing in these terrifying times to say nothing of the declining health of claiming stock. Also, he has been dead for quite a while, and I can hardly get directly at him for dialogue.

What must be taken to task, instead, are my own foolishness, gullibility, and vulnerable good nature which should have long passed with that time when I was able to place faith in easy answers. To believe in platers, I am trying to say, is like believing in virgins but only worse because there is no evidence that platers were ever anything else, even in the maiden-specials where most of them start, whereas for virginity at least there are certain precedents. I have seen young girls, public school girls, who I could clearly state were probable virgins.

According to Harry the Flat's special plater-system instructions, I selected a given plater, Silent Sun, a four-year-old $3500 claimer at the beginning of the season in Tropical Park because I liked his name and large ankles. I then played him faithfully all year. The principle is that he would finally win and in the process would enable me to recoup all of my losses with much excess since I would be doubling up my bets consistently. Meanwhile, the Mob who controls all the horse races, (I believed this at that time) would be working nicely with the horse's owners to make sure that when the animal won he would produce a fine price.

The heart of the system is that every plater must win once during a given year if he stays sound. That is because owners and trainers must bail out on what is essentially a losing proposition, since it costs so very much to keep a horse these days and bad horses act just the same as good ones in the eating and shoeing departments. Everyone's turn must therefore come in order to keep the wheel going. ("Racing is a wheel," Harry liked to say, "but this does-n't necessarily mean that it cannot come full circle.") It is important to say, however, that the given horse must stay sound in order for the system to pre-vail and one of the reasons platers are platers is because they are not celebrated for their good health, either.

Silent Sun, unfortunately, was beaten in eight straight races and then forced to retire for permanent repairs, due to a broken left tendon his front knee got, and which caused the trainer to have him shot most sympathetically in front of the stands at Aqueduct one fast but sloppy afternoon in July. Resultantly, I was never able to recover my losses since one of the eligibility requirements for a cheap plater race is that the horse at issue be alive at the time that his name is dropped into the entry box.

Silent Sun had several stablemates, of course, as is common with this kind of public training operation responsible for most of the platers, and one of them, I discovered, to my bewilderment, won and paid fifty-three eighty the very next afternoon. However, this did me no good, since, in tribute to the late Silent Sun I had spent all of that day mourning the deceased animal in the premises of Ferdie Lender, where I was trying to redeem a very shaky financial situation from the ruins.

"Consider," I said to Ferdie Lender, "it is true that the animal is dead but in March he won a race and would've paid over ninety-six dollars, except for the disqualification which knocked him back to fifth. Not only did I lose my money then, I suffered. Certainly I am entitled to some kind of support for this; the system works, it is only a matter of timing." Ferdie, however, was not particularly sympathetic, claiming various family troubles and missed round-robins which had temporarily sewn his funds up tight. At the root of it, I be-lieve that Ferdie has some connection with the Mob, himself, but this is an accusation which I could not possibly prove. Raising it without proof would only tend to hurt his feelings; beyond that constant aspect of pain which he wears like a sheath even now. "I cannot help you," he said, "even in memory of Harry the Flat and his system, I cannot give you the kind of backing you need. Of course, if you wanted me to book a few of your bets when you run the system again, that's something else. But, although I can be a sportsman, I can no longer be a financier; things have changed in the last few years and racing is no longer the same." He then offered me, for my diversion, a mod-estly-commissioned shot at his runner, Dorothy Wheels, if I wanted to for-get about business. This I had to decline. Long losing streaks tend to make me impotent, which is one of the reasons why my sexual life is somewhat spo-radic, even with people for whom I feel affection.

Therefore, I was in the hole for the tune of some one thousand, eight hun-dred and three dollars after this unhappy event occurred. Since I did not have this money but had, as a matter of fact, been forced to borrow most of it from the Mob at steadily increasing rates I was in very dire circumstances since the Mob had advised me that my credit was being cut off after the final loan and some means of repayment was now expected. The thought that Silent Sun would run into footing difficulties had never occurred to me.

After a few routing attempts, then, at minor evasion, I had to come to terms with the Mob in the person of Tony Winner. Tony Winner, I am led to understand, is only a minor functionary in the overall scheme but is important and respected enough to be permitted to handle matters such as this. The Mob, sad to say, fails to take emotional losses into account when attempting to settle its books and it also, contrary to popular legend, chases smaller amounts even harder than big ones since they are more visible. Tony Winner was acquainted with my pain but unwilling to take it as repayment.

I do say this, however: I do not blame Harry the Flat for any of these grievous problems which have overwhelmed me. By being in person, dead himself, he can be counted upon to have paid off all his dues. Also, I am simply thrilled to have the opportunity to do this one little favor for my old and trusted friend.

X

A GLIMPSE OF AQUEDUCT IN JUNE. THE NATURE OF THE TOTE, THE WELTER OF THE GRANDSTAND

It is a grim, bleak, blank track, this; it seems to have been slammed in colors out of concrete, only those hues—pasteboards, the drab color of tickets—relieve it at all but in their aspect of chewed and ruined candy, somehow only increase the depression, nail to the senses the poison that is in this still, rising air. It looks like a child's toy of a track, imagined to enormous size, lacking the context of maturity and it is instantly apperceptible in this obstacle of a shell that nothing can go on here that will have any tragic dimension whatsoever. No laughter, none of this, none of anything, only small, grim debacles and shame enacted over and again in some frozen graveyard of the spirit, a trick which seems to simultaneously propound and deny responsibility. A dream, a conception this thing, even an escape: call it a mental institution in which the inmates wander around in a kind of perpetual occupational therapy listening to the magnified drone of the Counselor telling them over six hundred speakers that everything will be all right, eventually, somehow, next race, could be. No changes. The tote glimmers and blinks, dazzles out its own messages to the crowd which have nothing to do with horses and in the bowels of the grandstand, in the swelter underneath the plane in which they sit, bodies are packed like fish in their density: mouths opening, gasping querulously, a flicker of newspaper, jot of sweat, a howl of rage the nearest one can come in the apprehension to those emotions which took one here in the first place to deposit him in this house of pulp.

Murder. Murder. Ah, Harry, there is murder here yet.

XI

THE POLITICAL THEORY OF
HARRY THE FLAT

Harry the Flat was at Aqueduct racetrack on the well-recollected 22nd of November, 1963 on which date John F. Kennedy, the beloved President of the entire United States was assassinated. The announcement of the President's severe medical problem was made by Fred Caposella over the public address system at one twenty-five p.m., just before the third race and the popular Fred M. Caposella added that the condition was still uncertain and all racing fans should pray for the health of the young President, to say nothing of his future, while standing by for bulletins. In the third race number six was two pounds over.

"Ha, ha! it ain't got nothing at all to do with the form charts," said Harry the Flat. "They're going to put this one over under the record, can't you see it?" and went to the window to make his bet. The horse on which he bet a hunch, New Times, was fourth in a tightly-bunched field, being unfairly crowded on both turns. "Fuck this shit," said Harry the Flat, "I need a winner, I got to get out of this, got to move along, otherwise it all ends up in the Dallas way," and went back to bet on Bob Lynn Sue in the fourth race. The information on this horse had been passed onto him by a tall Greek in the grandstand who said that he knew the owner personally and that the filly must win today, otherwise they were out of business. This information thrilled the Flat, not only because it let him onto a possible score, but because a tall Greek in the grandstand would think enough of him, a local stranger, to pass this word on. Just as he placed his bet he was informed, along with others, that John F. Kennedy, once the President of the United States, had died in Dallas just about twenty minutes ago because of certain peculiar, mortal wounds. Scurrying out to the infield to be part of all this excitement, sticking his cigar between his teeth, Harry the Flat joined the majority of the infield crowd in vigorous applause. Bouncing up and down with the exertion, his small features winding their way with intricacy to some point of conjoinment on his round face, Harry radiated much of the excitement which America must have felt at that moment. "Teach him, the son of a bitch," he said, "but then you can't win them all now, can you, really?" and went back to the window on a hunch to throw another twenty on Bob Lynn Sue to win since she had the same first name as some relative the President had . . . but this proved to be his truest and most unfortunate undoing since Bob Lynn Sue Placed but did not Win.

Harry blew the twenty he would have made on the original win-and-place bet by the extra stab. The missed tip, the maddening, elusive Greek who he wanted to straddle in rags and pulp, the high, clinging scent of ozone in the air, the blare of the megaphone, the glare of the sun, the news that they were going to cancel the program after the seventh, came together in Harry for his one, great political insight and he said, "The trouble is that something always gets between you; between you and it, and I'm not talking about fucking now, because the fucking you get simply ain't worth the fucking you take."

Several horseplayers looked at him with interest but there were no real comments.

XII

HOW HARRY DID IT TO HIMSELF

I think this is the way it happened: Harry the Flat committed suicide on June 19th, 1967 at Aqueduct racetrack, a fine, warm, late spring day in Ozone Park when the temperature was eighty-five degrees, the humidity thirty-one percent. This is how it must have been: the suicide occurred immediately after the fourth race when Rock Diver, let go at five to two, finished fifth in a seven horse field, unaided by blinkers and the enthusiastic and sexual pumpings of his jockey. "Son of a bitch," Harry must have said to the large crowd of friends and onlookers, including Tony Winner in the upper grandstand, "son of a bitch, I can't stand it anymore, I can't stand it! The system stinks, I see that now. Why did I ever get taken into this pursuit?" and without waiting for an answer removed a small point, twenty-two caliber pistol from the inner pocket of his plaid sports jacket, put it firmly against his sweating temple and pulled the trigger.

"Gee," I think he added, "that was stupid of me," just before the rictus of death, a curiously soundless explosion, overcame his now-smiling features and he plunged inert to the ground, a copy of Lawton protruding cheerlessly from his breast pocket. His death was curiously bloodless and artistic the way I think I remember it; a fact which more than any other permitted the Winner and other acquaintances to say as they considered his corpse that it was certainly a shame Harry had to go this way but on the other hand he could at least be granted a last wish often expressed to have Aqueduct as his final resting place.

"Bury him here right now," someone said and picking up the form, his friends conveyed him to a vacant Harry M. Stevens free-flow pushcart which had been abandoned by its vendor after the daily double; the pushcart and its horrid contents were then conveyed down the escalator, onto the lawn and in a few nimble but clamorous twitches across the rail. Then to the backstretch itself, I can see it now, so clear and distinct that it could have been in no other way, past a few indolent swans on the infield lake who looked at the excursion without interest but terrific knowledge.

Excavations were rapidly and successfully accomplished; Harry was joined to the turf which he had so judiciously calculated for most of his adult life and then his friends went off singing, if not drunken, into the bright remnants of the afternoon. "The least we could do for him" and "this should hold up the early speed a bit more" were among some of the comments passed, comments which seem rather indistinct in my mind, however.

As a matter of fact, it all seems indistinct: what happened is the only possible explanation for Harry's burial and I know that it must have been in this way but the Winner, among other abilities, has the talent of clouding men's minds and perhaps my memories of this are not all that they should be. Perhaps what we did was to wait with Harry until nightfall before burial. Or then again, I have a vague feeling that Harry might have dug his own grave out there and shot himself in solitude, maintaining only enough sentience in his ebbing life forces to cover himself up for ascending. One does not know. I cannot pursue explanations further. I have immediate, pressing business, and the present is all. It has been four years now, after all, and so much has happened since then.

The early speed did tend to hold up a bit during the next couple of days' racing, but by the end of the week, things had settled down to their usual dismal level and the Harry the Flat system, along with so many of the others, was also discarded. Harry would have been proud of the ability of his friends and acquaintances to discount his presence on the back-stretch once it proved unavailing. "Flexibility," he would caution us in his days on earth, "flexibility. Never stay with an angle if you can disentangle."

XIII

MY RELATIONSHIP WITH GERTRUDE NEE HAWKINS IS HEREIN EXPLAINED FOR THE VERY FIRST TIME

I have been in love with the remarkable Gertrude nee Hawkins for several years, ever since, in fact, the first time I met her in the company of Harry the Flat on their wedding day.

Harry and Gertrude were wed in the Hollis Avenue Sacred Shrine Union Church of the Sacramental and Beloved Divine reception room on a fine autumn afternoon, and as one of his oldest and closest I was invited to the wedding. This made me participate in the Bringing of Gifts, though I had not previously even glimpsed the bride who had always been kept concealed from the Flat's companions during the period of his courtship. Probably he wanted to lay off his bets and not let her know what kind of acquaintances he was having or not having luck with. Gertrude was then and is now a lovely female with matron-like breasts, full and wide, white and thick in the suddenness of repose and exposure. I dreamed often of the Flat's adventures in paradise until I was informed by her, during our second adulterous tryst, that he had not gone to bed with her more than fifteen times in the course of their marriage. Harry settled for fucking only when he had lost huge bets or felt himself, via an important tip, on the verge of the enormous rim of chance. And all of these events, to make them even less convenient, seemed to occur during the early morning hours, that time being the only period of day when Harry could find an erection.

"You see, you see, he just ain't geared that way," she reminded me, laving my guilt with the flow of desire below and thrust her complacent flesh skillfully into my clamorous mouth. Oh God, I could have died that way: the softness of her flesh entwined with memory; images of the madonna circling thickly into lust, her rising nipple plunging my throat like a dancer, all meaning, all sensation darkened to that high, bright flame of purpose as I probed and probed her again, muttering my Love, Harry's foolishment, the anguish of the machinery into whose pistons we had fallen, cut to ribbons, bright blood moving swiftly, circles of spreading dark, streaming to the floor.

XIV

FINALLY REVEALING HOW LAWTON IS
ABLE TO GIVE WINNERS AND
MAINTAIN THE ILLUSION OF
SUCCESS WHEN ACTUALLY
IF YOU PLAYED HIM
FAITHFULLY FOR A
FULL YEAR YOU
WOULD LOSE
EVERYTHING
THAT YOU
COULD OWE

Lawton gives two horses in each of the nine races. They are almost always the strong morning line favorites in their races and if they aren't favorites they will rapidly become so because of the pari-mutuel system and the wide distribution which all of Lawton's picks receive. Of these eighteen picks, then, four or five will win on a normal day since better than one third of favorites do win and favorites and second choices combined will win half the races. This means that Lawton can thusly claim twenty or thirty winners a week but the prices   are   short and he does not remind you that it is as well to lose two win bets on longshots blowing four dollars as to win on one out of two races-four bets-on favorites and collect three eighty. Lawton is thus another illustration of the principle of disequity in the universe. This principle has much to do with my current adventures at Aqueduct racetrack in Queens, New York.

Also, I have had it out for him for a long, long time and think that this is a good opportunity to get that one thing off my chest.

XV

A FEW WORDS FOR THE WIDOW

Harry the Flat signed a telegram which the crowd at Bailey's Bar & Grill in Brooklyn sent Jacqueline Kennedy, the international beauty, on the eve of her first husband's funeral. He was hanging around getting drunk, when the thing came up. When the collection was made, he felt that he could not stay out of it easily without generating certain unpleasant hostilities in a bar whose tab he needed badly to sustain. He was able, however, to short fifty cents on the split by claiming that he had no loose change.

WE ARE TRULY SORRY FOR WHAT HAS HAPPENED AND WISH YOU AND THE KIDS THE VERY BEST IN THESE TIMES AHEAD STOP KNOWING THAT YOUR STRENGTH AND SPIRIT WILL COMFORT YOU AND ALL AMERICANS ARE WITH YOU TOGETHER AT THIS HOUR OF TRAGEDY AND PAIN STOP FOR THE UNITED STATES, the telegram said and the very next day the Flat read about himself in the paper in a story which noted the flood of sympathetic telegrams pouring into the White House including not only messages from simple Americans but from dignitaries of politics and the arts. That almost made the whole thing worth the expense and he certainly *was* sympathetic, even though the goddamned funeral bombed out the whole Monday card . . . including several very interesting choices which Harry had been teaching himself to watch for several months.

XVI

CERTAIN FINANCIAL CONSIDERATIONS

The Ultimate Tip on Knockover, the horse, will pay three hundred dollars or more or Tony Winner is no longer a winner. I intend to place one hundred of my own sequestered dollars on this horse, the better to exacerbate the pleasure of the mission. It will be impossible for me to cash my tickets immediately after the race, unfortunately, since I shall be otherwise occupied with the details of disinterment. I will be able to cash them at the previous days' windows on the next day or the day after that and when I receive this money, I am not able to talk of what will become of me other than that my life will radically change and very possibly for the better.

Fifteen thousand dollars.

Fifteen thousand dollars back for my hundred—small reparation for where I have been and what I must do. The sum I need, to consummate my existence then and, for all I know, to begin a newer and more complicated way of life with the lovely Gertrude, *for* the lovely Gertrude.

For her and for myself. We have been running in this season of chances too long; too long, now the entries must be changed.

XVII

A CHAT WITH TONY WINNER

"But why do you want him dug up? He's been buried there quietly all those years; what's the difference? He could stay there until the year ten thousand; how would they ever know it? No one, no one at all could tell."

"No he couldn't. He got to get out of there, that stiff. He always loused us up; now even when he's dead you got no peace."

"Why?"

"You're not supposed to know why."

"But I'm entitled. Think of the risks I got to take here."

"That ain't no matter; you're just the messenger. The hard detail man we call it. If you were supposed to know, I'd tell you. They'd give me the orders because that's the system. I read all about it in this book about the Mob. It was very interesting. I never knew they worked that way."

"I'm entitled to something for the risks."

"So what? It's your problem; I'm not taking them so what the hell?"

"I ought to know."

"I told you, we got our orders. It's the higher ark. I'm not even sure that I know the reasons for it."

"Oh come on, Tony, be reasonable. I'd take it as a personal favor."

"Maybe I don't know."

"Sure you know."

"That was just a joke, okay. I'm an inside man; I know everything. I wouldn't kid you that way, it isn't fair. Of course I know, they tell me everything. They know who the Winner is."

"Tell me then."

"You really want to know?"

"What do you think?"

"Well, if I gotta say it then, he's lousing up the figures, that's what the stupid son of a bitch is doing."

"Huh? Who?"

"Who? That stinking bum, lying under the sod there. He's done something to the dirt, it don't come down even. He's screwing up all the figures, the past performances, he's making figuring impossible. They run over that backstretch and they gain two seconds, lose four seconds, start crossing over in front of the field. They can't tolerate the error no more. Probably he's been doing something to the turf when he started to decompose."

"The burial did this?"

"The burial, fuck the burial, I mean that stiff is lying in there and lousing up everything. For a while they could compensate: Billy Chart was able to figure out speed and windage and variables so we could take the stiff into consideration but since they done so much racing over the track with the dual meets and Belmont being out of action until so late and the December racing and everything, something's happened. The arrangements don't stick. It's getting unpredictable, goddamn it, and we got to get that loser out of here before he louses up everything. I'm telling you, we're having plenty trouble making any kind of results with that kind of stuff going on in there. And then where would we be? We ain't making no money off the conventional operations, they're all taxed and it's mostly public relations. The only area you get yourself a little edge is in the arrangements and now we can't be sure of nothing."

"That's really something."

"It sure is. You tell anyone you're wise, bum, or that I put you up there, I will blow your head off with a shotgun or more likely use some kind of good and efficient hammer which is more reliable if somewhat less cleaner."

"Then if that's so, I got one single question to ask you."

"You got one. Exactly one and no more. I hate to sound like a tough guy or anything but they really make things hell if you don't stand up to it. It's a whole policy."

"If the figures are loused up, how can you be sure you can put over this Knocker?"

"Knockover, dummy. The name of the horse is Knockover. What you got on your mind?"

"I meant Knockover. Couldn't the figures get loused up on that one too?"

"Sure," Tony Winner says, "that's a sure thing, of course it could. But if they do then you get good and loused up too, meaning that you ought to be very concerned and involved with what you're really there to do and the hell with the tip. Forget about the horse. Because everything is chance, life is a chance, and I am sitting in this chair right here this minute only because one bit of sperm won out over a couple billion others and the four guys who sat in this chair years previous had to resign owing to these tiny little accidents with their circulation."

XVIII

HARRY THE FLAT ON THE SUBWAY
SPECIAL ON THE MORNING OF
THE DAY HE CANCELLED
OUT OF IT

He will meet his friends at the track; he insists upon travelling there alone, because in no other way can he find the time to himself, to think. Now, the *Telegraph* folded on his lap—it is hopeless, he can find no spots, he has for the moment given up—he sits alone on a double seat, drawn in gracefully upon himself, a small man, not to say delicate in appearances. The seat could with ease have been occupied also by a very large woman, for some reason, however, that very person who entered the car at the Hoyt Street station and seemed about to sit next to him changed her mind at a critical instant and, instead, sits across from him in a tiny single seat, glaring uncomfortably, muttering, but unwilling to join Harry. She holds her glasses between the thumb and forefinger of her left hand, twirls them, looks at Harry with energetic hatred and he finds himself wondering vaguely if there is something wrong with him, something which makes strangers in public places seek other accommodations or pass him by sniffling quizzically. He thinks for an instant of leaning over and asking the woman why she hates him so but decides that he cannot, she might take him for insane, and this is something with which he cannot deal. Instead he thinks of Gertrude who not three hours ago permitted her smooth, bland warmth to lie quietly beside him, deep in sleep, small nestles of her hair turning gently with his breath. Surely, he thinks, if such a woman would lie next to him there can be nothing wrong with his public aspect; the large woman is obviously unstable and he, the Flat, has nothing to fear. He tries to fixate on Gertrude, to get down in his mind exactly what she looks like and how he feels about her, but it is too difficult, too painful for reasons too obscure to identify. So he returns to the *Telegraph* opening it to the entries for the fourth race, and for the seventh time that day spots the figures on Rock Diver, a four-year-old gelding. He has been in and out of spots with this horse for a year, now it is time for all losses to recoup and he is positive that even as the favorite today it will win. "It's got to win, I know it will win," he mumbles and involuntarily clasps his hand, the woman stares at him, the train lurches, a whiff of subway filth comes through a window and into his nostrils, panels away and he clutches for a handhold as the *Telegraph*, unheeded for the moment, slides to the floor and turns gently in the wind. *Rock Diver, Rock Diver*, Harry thinks and the lights in the car wink out at a momentary circuit-break; he stabs in the darkness at what looks like stars, the lights go on again, the train stumbles into daylight. Unhappily the Flat does not take these events as an omen which is one of the keys to his problem; for all his faith in mysticism, he has been selective about his anguries.

XIX

A BRIEF DIFFICULT MOMENT AT THE
ENTRANCE TO THE GRANDSTAND

I have driven out on the Long Island Expressway in a Mob Ford leased to me by Tony Winner, inasmuch as it has been agreed that the conveyance of spade and shovel on the subway special would be more conspicuous than truly desirable. Since the subway special is my usual habitat and accustomed means of travelling to Aqueduct it has been an uncomfortable drive, although the power steering and brakes on the Ford are considerably easier to manipulate than a subway strap. Tony Winner has thoughtfully provided a stereo tape collection of bugle calls and announcements of interesting races to hold my attention during the trip. Because of the nature of the mission, I have been compelled to put the car into the grandstand parking section and hike my way into the grandstand itself, the spade and shovel packed neatly into an excellent leatherette cello case which was given me by my sister a long time ago as an inducement to a musical education. Everything goes relatively well up to the time of paying admission, although several of the customers, walking in with me through the parking lot, want to know whether I am playing a cello concert on the grounds during the day and what selections on the cello would be the most appropriate for a very cheap card. Although I appreciate the humor of these remarks, and in different circumstances might have made some myself, I find that the best response to them at the present time is complete silence and disapproval. Music, although it has never been one of my great interests, is not to be sneered at and to be a concert cello player would be a fine and remarkable thing, although not strictly applicable to the picking of winners. At the window, however, when I extract my wallet to pay two dollars admission, a terrible thing happens: somehow, the zipper on the cello case becomes undone, or perhaps it was undone all the time. And from the opened case spill the two implements which, in gentler circumstances, have been referred to as gardening tools. They fall in the area of my feet with a dreadful clatter, managing to somehow stub the toe of a large blonde in attendance with a short, serious horseplayer type. "What the hell do you think you're doing, friend?" the short horseplayer type asks of me while the admissions clerk and ten or fifteen people on line eye the scene with interest. I cannot say that I blame them.

"Oh," I say, having never been particularly graceful at social banter, "Oh, I'm sorry. I don't know how that happened." I bend and snatch the two dreadful implements, trying to stuff them back into the cello case but in the heat of the moment and because of certain cross-angles I do not have entire success. The line begins to mutter and the admissions clerk seems to curse me, a most embarrassing interlude since whatever moderate success I've had in my forty-one years on this planet has come from making myself inconspicuous in most situations. "My toe, my toe," the blonde says and begins to poke and flex the member. "I think you really hurt it."

"You hurt her toe," the short horseplayer says and removes a cigar from his inner coat pocket which he places into his mouth with some concentration. "Did he hurt you bad?"

"He bruised it, can't you see?" she says, showing him something pink, not the only pink protrusion of female companion flesh since she is wearing a halter which shows off what she has to some slight advantage, "I mean, what kind of people are there in this place anyway, honey? Here I was thinking he was so sensitive and fine and all that. How many times do you see a cello player coming into Aqueduct and he turns out to be a bum who makes an attack upon my toe with his shovels? What do you think of that?"

"Yeah, what *do* you think of that, friend?" the horseplayer asks. What was an implicit inconvenience seems to be rupturing into a major confrontation and fear rushes through all of my stick-like limbs, to say nothing of my white cheeks and intelligent eyes. It is not physical fear of these circumstances so much as what I know will happen if Tony Winner gets wind of the way in which I have made my entrance to Aqueduct racetrack. For reasons which I have long felt to be obvious, Tony is a big fan of quiet entrances and exits. "I'm sorry about your toe, lady, I really am," I say, the tools at last snugly back into the cello case and the case neatly zipped. "I really didn't mean anything personal by it." Carrying the case tightly now, I could be a symphony instrumentalist, making my entrance into Carnegie Hall but somehow it does not carry as it should. People are giggling and the ticket seller has opened his window to look at me, with a distinctly unhappy expression. "My toe," she says again, "you really hurt my toe."

"What right you have calling my wife 'lady'?" the horseplayer says. "You think that you got to show some respect, do you?"

"I don't understand," I say, "I don't follow what you're saying."

"Pain," he says, "lots of pain can happen to men who make remarks like that. What are you staring like this for? Get a move on before I bend your guitar case over your pointed head."

Thankfully, I reach into my pocket to produce the two dollars which one way or the other will buy me out of the scene but I cannot escape one final disaster, the handle of the case slips from my hand and hits me a stinging blow on my own big toe, that very toe which I use to poise myself on at the finish during happier days, to cheer home a winner or at least a Place horse. The pain is astounding and I crumple with it, meanwhile becoming momentarily oblivious of my surroundings which turn out to contain not only the usual cast but two large, grim Pinkertons who eye me with suspicion and dread as I massage the appendage with the hand still containing the two crushed dollar bills. "I'm sorry," I find myself mumbling, "I'm really very sorry."

"Has he been a nuisance to you?" I hear the Pinkertons asking the blonde and at that instant I want to hear no more; counting upon the demeanor of the Pinkertons to say nothing of the distractions of the track I thrust my two dollars at the attendant. In astonishment he presses the catch that releases the gate and I whiz through, followed by the cello case. With much rapidity I make my way into the track proper, past the program stands, past the tipsheet stand, past the *Telegraph* stand, past even the famous and dedicated Sister Annie who sits by an entryway in full costume rattling her plate for the Sacred Sisters of Mercy in the Heart of Benevolence in the Chapel of the Little Holy Sisters of Triumph and Saint Anthony.

It is an excellent indication of my mental state that I have forgotten, on this of all days, to give Sister Annie a contribution. She stares after me as I scamper through the alleyway. I do not need sensory organs any more delicate than those in my back to partake of her look: composed of revulsion and dismay it fairly convulses her saintly little features as her eyes darken and glint in the sun. Sun in her eyes, sun over the parapet, a hint of sun over the toteboard as I take the stairs two at a time and find myself in the main level grandstand of Aqueduct racetrack and still a long, long way to go to the elevators.

It has been graceless but at least I am here and I induce myself to feel, true or not, that somehow Tony the Winner and his supporters would cheer. I decide that before I go one step further I deserve a drink, a single little drink, to carry me on my way and on my tragic mission.

XX

HARRY THE FLAT ON THE NEW
MORALITY

Prior to his marriage to Gertrude in the fall of 1960, Harry the Flat would occasionally frequent bars in the vicinity of Ozone Park and points east on winning weekday evenings. These neighborhood bars were apt, at any given time after nine p.m., to contain a large scattering of single girls, some escorted and some not, some seeking companionship and some not. The Flat was often the subject of amused and affectionate kidding from his friends because he steadfastly refused to become involved with any of these girls, even to the point of noticing their presence in the bar, much less buying them a drink. Since his reputation had spread along with his single-minded dedication to horse-racing in the years of the 1950s, this was not as easy it looked, inasmuch as the Flat from time to time, rumored large scores which would be of particular interest to some of these unescorted girls. When confronted by one of them, which might happen once or twice every six months, the Flat would upset his drink and scamper rapidly to the men's room in which cool spaces he might stay for minutes or hours until he felt the more immediate pressure-points had eased and he could safely make his exit. "What's wrong with you, why are you afraid of girls?" one of his acquaintances once asked him, being careful to add in the confidence of a rye-and-water that, of course, he did not suspect the Flat, even in the least of faggotry. Once this inference had been raised for kicks by the drunken Marvin Beers during the running of the third race at the old Belmont. The Flat, not otherwise known for physical accomplishments, had stopped witnessing the race long enough to destroy the helpless Beers, who had vomited most of his day's intake, to say nothing of his hopes darkly in the aisle, while their mutual selection ran fourth in a six-horse field. "I mean, they don't mean no harm, these here and they got their purposes."

"You do not understand," the Flat said, indicating with a shrug and a wink that he took no offense and that the question was safe, at least for the course of one evening, "I am saving myself for the time when I get married, which hopefully may be soon—just as soon as I can establish enough of a score to give my wife some security. The marriage is a holy and sacramental act in which sex can be beautiful to both of the participants but in addition to that, I think that these girls are very cheap and are just looking for superficial things, which I cannot give them, my attention being wrapped up elsewhere. I have too much respect for what women should be to pay any attention to the goings-on in Pop Warner's,"

"But they're easy, it's just a simple score," his friend pointed out, "and anyway it isn't as if Queens is the East Side, the price is right. You don't have to promote and they're simple enough to take it for what it's like. Not meaning any offense of course."

"It breaks your concentration," the Flat said, "the whole thing just shakes up the rhythm and this rhythm is very important to establish and to stay on with. They just use themselves and sex to distract you but if you let yourself get distracted then you can't accomplish nothing no more. Once you start getting involved it's just like chasing longshots, you get in deeper and deeper and you always think the next time is the last, but the fact is that you never get out. They won't leave you alone. Not having anything against women of course. I told you, I hope to get married just as soon as I can make some of the breakage."

"Well, that's your decision."

"It isn't a question of a decision, just noticing the way things have changed. Have you noticed how things have changed? These girls are a different type altogether from the way they used to be. I used to get involved you know. Before I got serious and really found out what I wanted to do in life, I chased around a lot. But these girls are different. They're more aggressive. They won't leave you alone. They're always hustling you for something, have you noticed?"

"I try not to pay too much attention to them myself," the friend said. "My feeling being that one takes one's drinking and one's sex at different times and places and in most bars the best thing for one to do is to drink."

"Well then you see my point. I don't know exactly what's happening but I see them all over now and they all seem to be the same. A lot of them come into the track with their boyfriends and the first thing they want is money to bet with and the second thing is that they have ideas exactly how to bet the double. It ain't no good. It's no good at all. I tell you, the whole thing has changed, it used to be that you could count on women being in one place and you being in another when you wanted to keep it separate but no more, no more. Someday, I tell you the truth, someday I can see it happening, we're even going to have girl jockeys. They'll be doing that too and once they get into the racetrack that way you know that we're all finished. But at least it will be a long, long time and I have the comfort of knowing that I shall be dead when this horrendous event comes to pass."

The friend and acquaintance was about to continue on the discussion raised by this horrifying possibility, when we were interrupted by the sudden entrance into the bar of two girls. They came trailing all the way down the length of the counter, stopped before the Flat, and said they had heard confidentially that he was the toughest rock on Queens Boulevard, and since they happened to be slightly drunk they would test this out for themselves. The larger of the two then attempted to kiss the Flat, precipitating a series of events which I will not discuss other than to say that in their intensity and polish they added up to some of the greatest moments the Flat had ever had. The consequences, although minor, seemed at the time to be totally past any kind of reasonable control for a long, long time.

"I can't stand it, I just can't stand it," the Flat said when at last the floor was cleared, "can't you see that I'm just trying to save my seed?"

XXI

A GLIMPSE AT MY BACKGROUND, SOME APPREHENSION OF THE KIND OF PERSON WHO MIGHT COME THIS WAY. INFERENTIAL TECHNIQUE BUT SO ARE SELECTIONS

Like most of my friends and acquaintances to say nothing of the celebrated Flat himself I did not come to my present occupation on a straight-line course like the way that a doctor or lawyer or architect tends to utilize the Pipeline Technique. Instead, like most horseplayers, I wandered my way back and forth, in and out, and finally kind of fell into it backwards and with a stunning and discovered sense of involvement. In this way and only in this way, I am led to understand, can horseplayers be compared to writers and some other people in the Creative Arts. In all other ways, they command a far more useful occupation and a more meaningful future.

"You've become totally irresponsible," the girl who was my wife stated. "I don't know what's happened to you but I don't like it. You're not the same and you do not even pretend to be. If this keeps on, I will have to get a divorce."

"I cannot be frightened by the prospect of divorces," I said to her, rearing up from the pillow and snatching a copy of the *Telegraph* from the adjoining night table. Whenever these discussions reached a certain peak, the girl who was my wife had a specific habit of attempting to destroy the *Telegraph*, which not only was a fifty cent investment shot but contained all of my figures for the following day. Hence, I had become protective. "Divorces are only a state of legality, it's a question of relationships which count. I told you, the fact that I have become interested in horses has nothing to do with my feelings to you, which remain the same. You must trust me."

"You have a good future. You've got to think of that future and children. We've got to have children and you're responsible to them. Don't think you'll find answers in that disgusting paper of yours."

"Now you have me being responsible to things that don't even exist," I pointed out to her, tucking the newspaper into a safe and unreachable place under the bed, "I have enough trouble being responsible to what is. You can't scare me with that kind of talk because it doesn't even matter anymore. Don't you see that the angle will work?"

"I don't even know what you're talking about!" she said and yanked the sheet from both of us, exposing her nude expanse which I note, parenthetically and in retrospect, was most enticing, but which had absolutely no momentary interest for me. "You keep on mumbling about systems and angles and charts and possibilities, but all I can see is that you're losing all of our hard-earned money. Don't give me any song and dance about how I don't know the figures, I see what's going on here. We're living on my salary now, yours is going down the drain every week."

"It just takes a little time to break in," I observed. "You can't come into a game cold and beat the hell out of it anymore than you can start off in politics as President. It takes time. Believe me, everything will shape up. The system is infallible and I'm starting to get it."

"You're totally irresponsible," she said, flinging the covers at me and rising to her full, lithe height of five feet six inches. She then leaped off the bed like a swan and beginning to stride around the room, the very vigorousness of her exercise not concealing from me the fact that she had no idea what she was doing. "Totally irresponsible, and the thing is that you have potential, you could make something of yourself."

"Now you listen to me," I said, similarly striding to full height and capturing her somewhere in the vicinity of the mirror. From that aspect I pinned her arms and forced her to look at the two of us in the streaked glass, forms wavering whitely in the fluorescence, "You listen to me because just this once I am going to say it and short and sweetly and I will not repeat myself. I do not want to hear about responsibility and potential. I do not want to hear about either one of these two important qualities because it is responsible people with potential who have gotten us exactly in the condition we are in now. It is responsible people who have been elected to the government, responsible people who are running the corporations, people with potential who have their hands on America, and you can see where all of this has gotten us. We have been put exactly where we are by sane, responsible men who meet their obligations in an approved way and I do not, speaking personally, want any part of it. It is time for a little irresponsibility, a little reality, if you will, and that is what I am after now. If you want to go along with me you will find that in the long run things will work out better and more sensibly this way. But if you don't want to go along with me, I should point out that I lived in the theoretically divorced state for almost twenty-two years before I made your acquaintance, and that can be returned to without any great sense of loss on my part. Now it is your decision but I no longer want to hear easy phrases, because I do not think you know what you are talking about."

"Oh," she said, "Oh you," and only then did I realize that during the latter part of this dialogue she had been moving against me, pushing her buttocks against my steadily erecting genitals which responded to my rhetoric in their own fashion. She was grinding her little ass against me as if the prick was the flame and she the moth and unresistingly I slid my hands to her breasts and began to touch them, press them, indent them. "Oh you're impossible," she said, "you're impossible, I can't take it any more," but the body was talking its own dialogue, the body was making its own adjustments, its own connection in the sudden and stinging dark. Lunging into one another we made slow transverse toward the bed and on the bed we fell into one another the way that two horses, one lugging in, can connect near the rail in a tight race. Try as I could to suppress images of horses from my mind they rose with the other heat, blended with the other necessity and that is the way I took her for the next-to-last time, lunging again and again toward the toteboard of her body, watching the crazy-lights flicker as I plunged endlessly into and around her hole. Finally, the lights went out altogether as I drove past the finish wire thinking of the responsible men, the generations of responsible men who had taken us here, all of them tight-faced and stunned against the dark as the final sense of it began to come slowly home toward them. "Crazy, you're crazy," the girl who became my ex-wife said, and in the aftermath of orgasm, drained and stricken myself, I could say nothing but "I had to, I had to," until I began to believe it myself. The sheets were sliding like snakes under us, the dazzle of summer insects in the air somehow in their fluorescent, encompassing buzz making artifacts of the two of us as I made what accommodation I could in the descending and sensuous night.

XXII

A DRINK FOR OLD TIME'S SAKE BEFORE
THE FIRST. ETERNAL RE-ENACTMENT
IN THE GLOW OF THE INNER TOTE.
A BARTENDER WHO ONLY WANTS
TO HELP. A TIP THAT MUST
BE GIVEN.

At the bar I order a Whiskey Sour straight up and check the odds on the inner tote while the bartender gets the drink. It is one eleven, only nineteen minutes until the first race and the number three horse, eight to five, appears to be the favorite but my sense of time, to say nothing of selection, has been suspended by the astonishing events of a few moments past and I conclude that I am highly entitled to the drink that I am about to get. The fact that this may be a rationalization means as little to me as the knowledge that in some three and a half hours, a mere two hundred minutes from now, I will be deep into the profound act of disinterment. All of it is too abstract. The bar is surprisingly empty for the time of day at Aqueduct and I am treated to an unobstructed view of my bartender's neck and shoulders as, busily, he suits himself to obtain my pleasure.

He is my bartender because in the six or seven months since he has joined the Harry M. Stevens Institute and administered to me behind the grandstand bar, which has been my own special enclave for some years, he has given me a daily double selection each and every day. This bartender, whose name is Alexander, spots one double pick every day as a means, he says, of supplementing his wages from the cheapest corporation in the modern western world. Although in all this time not a single one of these selections has hit or even come close, he still passes them on to me with an intimate and dreadful kind of confidence along with the first beer. "You'll see, you'll see," he says, "they come in and pay a mint and I'll be all straightened out nicely. You want to hear from me what happened in Latonia?" and he goes on to tell me, the same story repeatedly. It's about when he was a singles man at Latonia Downs, not too many years ago, his 9-6 double came in to the tune of three thousand and eighty six dollars, this sum being sufficient to finance him in the opening of his own bar & grill outside Thistledown Park. The bar & grill failed after a time, along with most of the Thistledown chalk, but Alexander the bartender, now back in the concession business, still is way ahead of the game and is willing, the higher virtue, to share his knowledge with me. Now as he puts the beer before me in a glass gently steaming with curls of ice and Harry M. Stevens refrigeration he says, "I got a good one for you today, the real thing, the real article. What's with that guitar case? You play with the band?"

"No," I say, "my sister takes cello lessons at the Juilliard Institute but was forced to go to a social event uptown today to which she could not bring her cello. Her lesson is at seven this evening and I will meet her outside of the Lincoln Center with this very excellent cello which she will then proceed to play and play. Speaking for myself, however, the musical gift in the family is specific rather than general and I can't make a sound with it."

"Well, that's very interesting," he says. "Personally, however, I am a great lover of music when the Seuffert band comes to play for us on spring Saturdays. So take no offense."

"There are no cellos in a band," I say, knocking off the beer with a dazed sense of completion and pushing across to him the mandatory fifty cents which is my greeting tip, "a cello is an orchestral instrument like with the one hundred and one strings or the Hollywood Bowl."

"Nevertheless," he says, pocketing the tip and rattling the coins in his apron until a slow, stupid grin of satisfaction spreads over his oval face; I hate to say it but Alexander, the Stevens' bartender, is not the brightest of persons, being, as too many limited people are, more addicted to the feel of money than its symbolic purposes, "nevertheless, I have something for you. I got it from a very 'in' source. It's the best information I've heard in weeks."

"I'm laying off the double today," I say, which is completely the truth, since I have not bet any of Alexander's picks since the first disastrous weeks. "Actually, I'm just kind of here for some fresh air; there's nothing really good on the card."

"Sure there is," he says, "nine winners, and besides that, I got this information from a very privileged source and you must not let it get around. This is no double. This has nothing to do with the doubles, it's in the eighth race."

"The eighth?"

"Exactly, the eighth. Now listen to me and remember who it came from because personally I am going to bet the horse ten and ten, ten to win and ten to place and this would be one of the largest bets I have ever made on a horse in my life, excepting that one time in Latonia. Do you want another beer?"

"All right," I say, feeling the horrid pressure of the cello case now digging me meanly in the hip as I shift my weight; meanwhile fighting off the dismal feeling that once again the case is attracting somewhat of an excess of comment. "If you want."

"Sure," he says and gets me one from behind the counter, pours it into the cup two-handed, staring at it with enormous concentration, slight wrinkles and twitches appearing over his forehead. "Warm in here," he says, "no pleasant environment."

"I am still waiting to hear about this tip," I say, passing Alexander a dollar and waving away the change.

"Oh sure, sure," he says, putting the bill into his apron—I suspect that he is working this one off the register—"I just wanted to know that you were really interested. The horse came from the most inside of sources—who, I cannot reveal. It is a horse named Knockover."

"Knockover," I say and regret to add that a slight dislocating tremor causes me to tilt the cup and pour a small but upsetting quantity of beer over my right pants leg. "Knockerover?"

"No," Alexander says tolerantly, producing a bar cloth and tenderly wiping the counter, "no, just Knockover, that's all. Surprised a little bit at this, are you?"

"Oh no, no, how could I be? I never really think I noticed the horse."

"Well, you might be surprised; you'd have a right to be. He figures to be at least eighty to one, even after the inside action. The horse hasn't won in two years, not since a maiden race at the Fairgrounds and he didn't even win that one. He was third and there was a double disqualification. His figures are terrible. But I got word."

"It don't figure," I say, trying to retain my cool and some quantity of Harry M. Stevens beer which seems to be moving around my insides rather unevenly; the fact of the matter seems to be a minimal but definite nausea. "It simply don't figure."

"Well," Alexander says and shrugs, "of course it don't figure but neither did the burning of Belmont. As I say, I got it from a very strong source. If I didn't trust you I wouldn't even spread it. Don't let it get around."

"Oh no," I say, "no, I won't. I'll sit on it tight," and at that moment three or four horseplayers, it is hard to make out numbers, approach the bar talking in Spanish about some of the jockeys, looking at my cello case with uneven, lascivious glances and I decide that it is time for me to make my exit. I seize the case, clamp it tightly under a shoulder, feeling it prod like a piece of deadly armament against me and putting another dollar bill on the counter for the sake of Alexander, I make my way away from the bar, into the open area and finally toward the escalator. Through all of this I move through another forest of glances toward my equipment but I now pay them no heed; my mind is far away, my mind in fact is on other matters entirely. My mind, to tell the truth, is occupied with a hundred different issues or at least one of them and I see nothing whatsoever as swaddled within myself I ride in stately fashion up the escalator toward the roof of the grandstand.

I am not sure exactly why I have left the extra dollar bill for Alexander but I suspect and have reason to trust my instincts, that it has to do with a decision I will shortly make, never to see him again. Whether this applies to Alexander specifically or the establishment in which he works, generally, is something I am not prepared to tackle directly at this time but I know that that too will come, will come, will as all things, percolate slowly, and then flower like a bullet within me.

It is all strange and with one hand I fumble in the inner coat pocket for a program to check whether Knockover's morning line odds remain at the cheerful fifty to one printed in the morning paper. Too late I remember that I have not yet bought a program and am thus caught in frieze on that escalator, one eye cocked toward my chest, the other blinking away sudden water, gracelessly poised in the act of diving into myself only to come up, like so many horses and jockeys I have seen, empty.

XXIII

SNAPSHOT: HARRY THE FLAT WATCHES A LONG ONE COME IN, A PARLAY COLLAPSES, THE NIGHT QUICKENS

Stretched on the rail now, hunched into a dwarf's posture, the heat of the crowd knifing him against himself, the Flat's concentration seems to have dwindled into a small pinpoint, a gleaming tunnel of light squeezed on all sides pressure from within and without. His horse, the six horse, is still on the lead as they stagger toward him around the stretch turn, the six beginning to stumble in the mud, heave for breath but nevertheless retaining three lengths over the rest of the claimers. The horse's eyes, Harry thinks, are somehow bright with anguish and cunning as it struggles thickly to do what is asked of it. It is only a furlong to the wire, maybe a little less, three lengths to hold onto and if the horse can hold, it will pay seventy two or seventy three dollars, seven hundred and twenty or thirty to the twenty the Flat has on him. In addition it will nail down the second third of a modified parlay which the Flat was up until three o'clock this morning doping out as he lay twitching in bed in a posture of consideration past the dawn. *Son of a bitch, son of a bitch,* the Flat murmurs, seeing the horse weave toward the rail and then shy in dismay, *they ain't got no fucking right to do this to me,* understanding, not for the first time at all that it has been madness, madness. He has turned over his life and any sense of its control to beasts which are utterly mad, utterly beyond influence and as he thinks this, something tickles at the base of his scalp, wants badly to be thought. He chases vaguely after the thought which (he realizes) will be very important to him but too late, too late for any of that thinking nonsense, the horses are coming by him now and the six is in deep trouble. A horse on the outside has hooked it on the rail and the six is stumbling, spitting, showing all the signs of a horse which has been whipped. "Oh for God's sake!" the Flat murmurs, "please, a little more, just a little more," and perhaps the horse hears him and perhaps it does not. It gears up for one final effort and breaks its right foreleg, the cannon bone, right above the knee, and falls flopping, fish-like to the ground. The other horses go by. The Flat and the six horse confront one another in a seemingly infinite expanse of acreage, the jockey thrashing on the ground in pain, his own cannon bone seemingly destroyed and numbers begin to go up on the board as the six horse, shaking its head, stumbles to its feet and swaying, attempts to finish the race on three legs.

"Crazy, crazy," the Flat mutters because watching this the thought which he had pushed away assaults him full force and although he cannot verbalize it at all he understands almost everything or feels he does. "It just doesn't make much sense," he adds with a near-boyish confusion as the jockey, twitching, his face grey, stumbles to his feet and starts to hop away. The horse whinnies, the crowd cheers, the hackers' truck comes with the rifleman, and the announcer, God bless him for his omnipresence, says that in the sixth race there are no changes and post-time for the sixth race is four oh two.

"Shoot him dead," says Harry the Flat, "the whole fucking parlay is right out the window."

XXIV

SOME SIMULACRUM OF HISTORY.
SOME SENSE OF REITERATION

Hovering over Gertrude, easing myself into her with slow, burning thrusts that seem to move her above as well as below, watching her face change in the receding light I find myself thinking of the girl who was my wife. It is the first time I think of her in several months or years but some aspect of illumination, some hint of tension around Gertrude's eyes remind me of her. I realize then that one of the factors which has always rendered Gertrude so appealing to me is this resemblance. In certain postures, at certain times she could indeed be my wife and perhaps it is this and not longing more direct which has sent me to her. I do not know. There is no way to be sure. Pounding in those crevices in which the Flat has dwelt once or twice in his lifetime, I find myself thinking of him too and my orgasm, seizing me like a noose, is bitter, bitter, winding and full. I pour into her, groaning all of the lamps of my love, and then hover there for a while as she comes back at me. Her orgasm, as always, is reciprocal to my own, known only as an aftertaste and response and it is hard, hard to maintain myself within her but I know that I must. "You, you," she says, just as my wife used to call my name in her own heat and I reach down, touch her nipples like a penitent, waft my hands over all the surfaces of her body and finally tumble, tumble, fall to her left side, crouching on the bed, reaching as always for the cigarette that will mean finality. As if she were unaware of my leaving her she moves on the bed in concentration, squeezing her thighs, her eyes closed and I feel that I should, as I did with my wife, put a finger into her to finish her off but again cannot do it; cannot accept deceptions on any level and so instead only work on the cigarette, tonguing it slowly like a nipple, watching the sun come fully into Gertrude's room. Strange and distant, distant and complete to understand that Gertrude embraces some forgotten necessity for my wife and I try to embrace the thought, accommodate myself to it but her hand is on my genitals, clamping away. After a time I turn back and do what I must, thinking small, gloomy retracted thoughts of maidens and platers and odds-scheme, two demented flies battering one another in the lamp somehow fixating all of my consciousness, if not desire.

"Horseplayers," Gertrude says after a long time, "horseplayers. Is it true that you're thinking of it all the time? Can't you get your mind off that stuff for one second? I mean I understand how involved you can get and how interesting the whole sport can be but don't you think you could pay a little attention? There are lots of things that I could think about too you know but I try to show some decency."

Snorting clouds of smoke, adjusting my thighs more loosely on the bed, I begin to understand that my relationship with Gertrude may be edging into a sea-change and that something critical may have to be done if I wish to maintain it. The thought titillates me, although hardly in the more conventional sense and I chase it down an alley or two briefly. But the alley turns into the straightway at Shenandoah Downs and on that flat the horses scamper joyously, free at last. I close my eyes, the cigarette turned to ash, and dream and dream that afternoon of a week ago away.

XXV

THE GENERATION GAP AS ARTICULATED IN THE TIPSHEET BUSINESS. PATERFAMILIAS DEPLORED. YOUTH AS IT ENABLES RISK

Rumor has it that two of the top turf-sheet experts have not only their skill with the horses in common but are father and son: specifically the rumor is that the George Lawton who writes the selections for the New York Turf Letter is the one and only son of the well-respected Clocker Lawton who is the author of Lawton's Orange Sheet. If so, and there is no reason to disbelieve this rumor since it is the very excellent Billy Chart himself who is responsible for its forgatherance and credibility, it leads to many interesting reflections and possibilities because the two Lawtons disagree all the time and also have an entirely different way of regarding the races.

In the first place, Lawton's Orange Sheet is sold for seventy-five cents while the New York Turf Letter goes for one dollar and five, tax included. Also, the Orange Sheet is merely a slip of paper with the horses on one side and a picture of Lawton on the other telling his record for the year previous, which is always very good. Whereas the Turf Letter is red, white and blue and comes sealed into its very own envelope which contains no writings of any sort. The front of the Turf Letter contains the selections and a few tips on how to bet them while the back is entirely blank. The younger Lawton perhaps believes that his selections are their own reward and that no public relations are necessary.

But this is not the half of it as any regular patron of the two important tip sheets will swear to. It was Harry the Flat who pointed out almost ten years ago that it looked like the father was giving the chalk while the son was giving the longshots and he suggested that it came from a desire of the two relatives to cover all possibilities in several ways. Certainly, the New York Turf Letter, particularly in the cheaper races on the card, would almost always spot longshots at or near the top while most of the Lawton horses seemed to be always closing at eight to five. But this in itself was not precisely the point; the point was that every now and then the two letters would give the same horses in approximately the same order. It was these instances, never more than one a day but less than three a week, which led me slowly toward the Insight and that Insight was that the father and son, who loved each other basically very much, were having a big quarrel but would take time out from the quarrel every now and then, just to indicate that their feelings were in the same place. It was as if the younger Lawton, with all the impetuosity and bravery of youth was showing up the old man in his willingness to take flyers. The old man showed the stolid lessons of a lifetime but both of them had a weakness for unraced shippers and both believed firmly in the principle of the Single Gelding in the All-Colt Race. It was an argument, of course, that the Flat and Billy Chart suspected would never be settled but there were enough signs of accommodation, now and then, to indicate that father and son, in the long run, might be able to get out of it together and alive.

But in the meantime, the quarrel, like so many other quarrels, still seems without solution. In one sense it is settled because Lawton the Clocker picks more winners and sells four times as many copies of his Orange Sheets as the New York Turf but then the New York Turf sells for thirty cents more and has a very devoted if limited audience of its own. Also, enough of its longshots will come in to give it only a very modest proportionate loss over a season and sustain Lawton the George's argument that a modified progression will always get a player out.

Only one last problem remains. It is contained in an issue raised by George Needles, who in his capacity as resident medicologist for most of the people with whom I am associated, is both insensitive and stupid about the horse-races. As a matter of fact, George Needles has not, to my knowledge, made a single bet on a horse-race since his time of flunking out from medical school, over forty years ago, and compulsively refuses to read the *Telegraph* inasmuch as the figures give him a headache and his wife objects to the decor. His arguments, therefore, can be assumed to come out of the arrogance of misunderstanding. Yet it was Needles himself who suggested that the father-son question was merely a cover story for the Lawtons and that actually it was just one of them, one Lawton that is to say, who was talking out of the two sides of his mouth on every question, creating two personalities with two distinct points of view, so that no matter what happened on a given day, sales of tipsheets overall could not go down. If longshots won Lawton was covered through the George and if the chalk came in the Clocker himself would register a small but gratifying increase in the next day's sale. The use of two personalities in one tipster, George Needles' theory went, meant that almost any eventuality, including dead heats, was well-covered. "As a matter of fact," he added at the time he propounded this to us in the pleasant but unremunerative circumstances of a Blarney Rose at midnight, "if you want me to tell you something, just making a guess you don't understand, I'm not even sure that the guy's name is Lawton. It could be Smith or Beal or Goldstein or something like that. But Lawton has a nice ring, it sounds like authority and truth and the police, a ton of law, you get me? and anyway it means that he won't get no calls at midnight telling him how he screwed up on somebody's rent or obstetrical money. I wouldn't be surprised if that were the case. Why should you trust any of these guys at the track? I did it just once and as a result of this I am not a top-flight surgeon in the East working with neurology schemes but instead a very different kind of circumstance entirely, which is not to say you understand that I am knocking it or that neurology is so particularly fascinating."

But this we could not take. The doppelganger theory, the simultaneous inhabiting of two persona by one mad but cautious individual engaged in self-protection was bad enough but barely within the scheme of possibility. Worse things than this have been known to happen even in top and honestly-meant stakes races. But the inference that Lawton was not named Lawton, that there was not behind the orange, the red, the white and the blue some clear identity which could, in the last analysis be dealt with if everything collapsed, some living individual who functioned for all of us now and then as an imaginary court of appeal, this was too much. It was too much if Lawton were not really named Lawton because if he lied about something like that, then he could lie about everything.

So we took out George Needles from the Blarney Rose and gave him a little education and sent him home a chastened man. But as to what good it did and whether it affected George in the long run, I cannot possibly say, being too dependent upon him, ironically at this moment, to perform certain delicate adjustments which will be necessary within eleven hours if I ever want to dream of Lawton again.

XXVI

THE FIRST RACE. A FORETASTE
OF ECSTASY AND DOOM

At length I find myself in the upper reaches of the upper grandstand which will be my place of assembly during the entire day, up to the point of my assault upon the turf. It is not at Tony Winner's suggestion that I have selected this spot, he having rather left the question open, except to suggest that it would be worth my while to be at the track from the very opening of the card so that there would be no possibility of getting impeded sometime before the moment of connection. Winner is actually rather flexible. One could not, I have come to understand, have achieved his rather high and mysterious state unless one is willing to make adjustments—and he even left the question of the concealment of the implements to me. But just as the cello case seemed to make consummate sense when I borrowed it from my sister, so, similarly, the upper grandstand seems to make sense now. Not my usual post along the rail (which I have occupied for over four years as a tribute to the late Harry the Flat) because the possibilities of concealment would seem to be better with height and distance and also the tools are very cumbersome. They feel, more and more, as if they were going to spring out of the case in a series of deadly cleaving gestures which, for all I know, might emasculate people or effeminate them, depending upon one's point of view. It is in the upper grandstand therefore, that I now sit, suspended at some high angle, only the corner of the tote visible in this westernmost seat poised over the stretch turn. It is one twenty-nine, one minute before post, and the horses, whose numbers if not appearance I know very well, are being fed into the starting gate.

Through the excellent pair of binoculars, which I purchased with my first winnings some years ago, I scan the goings-on at the gate. It is a six-furlong race and I can spot the place where Harry is buried just a hundred yards or so up front from the gate; framed in the binoculars it can be seen as a slight discoloration of the dirt, hardly noticeable except to those already attuned Flatward but in that pinpoint of connection, that small slice of light coming through the glass it is obvious that it is a definite discoloration indeed, or possibly even a luminescence. Unquestionably something of this distracting nature could affect the break of the horses, to say nothing of their eventual performance. As I look at this it occurs to me, perhaps for the very first time, that Tony Winner and his cohorts are serious. They mean business. I am genuinely expected to remove the Flat from this space and bring him to another resting place. Before this moment, I now see, I had approached these activities in the same spirit in which I used to approach the racetrack; the question of losses or involvements was not serious because surely if the losses were noteworthy, my money would be refunded upon appeal. It seemed impossible to me that a fine and legitimate state like New York, presided over by an excellent and responsible Republican administration, could possibly be party to an experience which would tap out a man seriously and ruin his life. At the heart of it I was sure that a reasonable letter, spelling out all the difficulties and background, would certainly turn the trick. Sooner or later I came to realize that this was not so and that New York State no less than Nelson Rockefeller thought of me as an essential abstraction. It was this attitude which took me through my first two thousand of losses and by that time I had achieved a cynicism which made me feel that I could work it through on my own . . . that New York State might someday write *me* letters inquiring as to my interest in refunding winnings so that the mental hospital program could continue. The evolution of the horseplayer is an interesting study, not to be touched in these plain and simple facts which I am setting down in the form of a memory book, but someone of more skill than me should someday do the job. It is a fraud and a pity that not one single journalist writing about the splendid sport of horse-racing appears to be very literate.

Looking at the mound and now away I understand that Winner is serious, it is not a joke: the Flat is out there and they want him back. Surely, I, less than almost anybody at Aqueduct racetrack, should doubt the convictions of the people who have sent me there and the presence of the Flat: still, somehow, it becomes apparent to me that I have. Even hustling the Flat's body through the darkness, scent of grass and the urine of horses coursing through my nostrils four years ago, I was not truly believing. I thought that it was only a device or an imagining and that the Flat, like so many of his tips, would have no substance or meaning after his perishment. Still, there he is and quite a bit of trouble in the bargain. At the clang of the gate the horses come out poised in a stiff file, noses strained alertly toward the breeze, a panorama of attention and commitment rarely seen anywhere else. Then as they hit the Flatship a few strides out, the line begins to break, wander, and two of the horses caught in the middle of the pack seem to be in nothing less than severe trouble as, knocked off stride, they fold to the rear of the pack and inspect clouds through the slots in their blinkers.

It has not been my intention to make this a betting day, not up until the eighth anyway, but some hard core of purpose within me, some sportsman-like facility, demands that I have something on every single race ever run on the track in front of me on the off-chance that I might have picked a winner. There is nothing like the frustration of having the horse you would have bet come in first. It adds an element of the truly diabolical to the sport or as Billy Chart once put it, in a rather high-class fashion, it "increases the projective elements." Nothing gives me more dread than the fear of my elements becoming too projective and so I make my bets in all circumstances, circumstances which often are so confusing and maddening that the sum of a night's work on the race has assured me that nothing can possibly win it. But projective elements might do something very bad to me, it not only has a medical (as George Needles pointed out) connotation but somehow a vaguely sexual one and so the bets go in. In the present case, the first race at Aqueduct on Tuesday, June 9, 1971, I have bet five dollars on the number eleven horse, Royal Return, to place and ten dollars on the field horses numbers twelve, thirteen, fourteen and fifteen to win. The number eleven is a very strong horse, eight to five in the morning line and he should at least definitely place. As far as the field, I am getting four horses for the price of one, four horses going off at the splendid odds of seventeen to one and in a large field composed of poor horses—the race is for maiden fillies three years old and up—any one of a number of things can happen, rendering a four-way longshot an excellent bet. At least this has been my philosophy. I have not this one time, and for understandable reasons, studied the card particularly intently on the previous night and thus my ego is less bound with the results of the race than usual. Also, Tony Winner has kindly provided me with twenty-five dollars betting money, which money is to be considered the car expense account but which can be used in any way which seems fitting. My plan is to win out or lose the twenty five as soon as possible and in any case to then bring my own rather substantial financial resources into the picture by no later than the fifth race or time enough to get warmed up before the central eighth. I have taken three hundred and forty-eight dollars, my total assets, painfully secreted and kept away from any question of the Mob and it is these resources which are critical. What the Mob has given me is merely excess which must be treated with contempt, this being my theory, but what happens to me is the thing that happens to me during every race I have ever watched. All of this speculation and detachment to the contrary, in other words, I become almost frantically involved and by the time the horses hit the head of the stretch I believe, once again, that I am possessed of a very special destiny, known only to me and working through all levels of connection and that this race, like all the other races, addresses this destiny. This is neither sane nor profitable thinking and is certainly no way to make a serious dent on the sport of kings but nevertheless it is my approach. The cello case, to say nothing of its possessions huddled embryonically within, is forgotten. Only a slight bulging pressure against my calf, which I maintain, links me to the grandstand at all as the horses spread across the track and begin their final run for the four thousand two hundred dollar purse which is now the minimum in New York, thanks to the horsemen's strike of some years ago on behalf of their livestock which they felt to be unfairly abused.

I follow them with the binoculars, feeling myself twisted into some agonized posture of attention. The eleven horse is clearly beaten, some five or six lengths in back of the first flight and stopping, having lost his early speed which is exactly opposite to my calculations and expectations. Nevertheless there is a good deal to hope for because the thirteen and fourteen horses are coming on the outside with a good deal of purpose and the twelve horse itself is fighting for the lead with the number two. One hundred and seventy dollars for ten if things can hold up in this fashion, nothing exceptional but a fine tribute to my ability as well as the first winning bet which I will have cashed in nine or ten races. "Come on, come on," I find myself shouting, losing once again all sense of removal and propriety in the scent of money. I think of the Flat, who at certain tense moments would scream obscenities and sing jingles, lapses which at least I have never maintained and the twelve horse quits suddenly, throwing its head up like a virgin being felt underneath her skirts for the first time and repeating, losing its action, cantering gracelessly sidewise toward the rail and one would hope oblivion. The two is left on its own whipping and driving but the thirteen and fourteen are still with the pace, their jockeys too frightened or stupid to know that the two has put it away. Everything now funnels down into a telescope, the events as deadly and contained as if they were artifacts on a distant planet. In that removal I see the thirteen take cognizance of its number and bolt slightly toward the outer rail, just enough to throw the race (but the jockey must have lost control; horses never throw races as clumsily as that, not at Aqueduct racetrack). Now it is solely a matter of the fourteen which strains and strains, moves within half a lap of the two, moves within a neck's distance, moves to a nose and then a head advantage but the last two are past the wire, the margin at the wire, that is to say, being a neck which means that the two horse has unofficially won the race and officially as well since ninety-eight of every one hundred winners in New York stay up on the board. The jockey on the fourteen, a sixteen year old apprentice, shakes his head and grabs the reins as they go around the turn, muttering to himself. Through the binoculars we exchange a single, hopeless look of loathing which I know I will be making more of than he and then I put the binoculars down, gasping, white with sweat, open to the heat and sit on the hard wood, the cello case falling limply across my lap like a woman. I fold my hand around the place where the breasts would be. No comfort. No comfort.

The two, another longshot, pays thirty-eight forty, twenty-six sixty and seven eighty across the board. The place horse, one of the field, pays fourteen sixty and six eighty to show. I have, however, bet straight win only as instructed by all the instructors of handicapping this important and fascinating sport. Therefore I can only comfort myself with the knowledge that the place and show payoffs are disproportionate to the win. While the win bettor battles only a seventeen percent takeout, the place and show are often fighting margins approaching fifty. This is instructive and helpful since the fact that a ten dollar place bet on the field would have paid me a profit of some sixty dollars would be otherwise disturbing, disturbing if I did not know that I had been shrewd and careful and had as always played with the odds on my side.

The first race is over and has thus cost me fifteen dollars, slightly more than my average per race but close enough to the norm to once again drive home to me the fact that the disastrous losing streak is not yet over, that it might never be over, that I need all the help, not to say alterations in personal circumstance that I can get. It is probably best that something dramatic will occur today to yank me permanently, one would hope, from this grim and terrible course. It is only in the moments immediately after a losing race that I can face what I push off at any other given time and that is twofold: that I am extremely mortal and that I am a lousy horseplayer. In some careful way these two seem to be connected but not so that I can make much sense of it. I do not think, for instance, that I would necessarily be a better horseplayer if I were immortal, only perhaps somewhat of a more patient one.

I put down my binoculars and turn around stiffly to look at the people surrounding me in the grandstand, once again aware of circumstances and the pressure of the cello case which I dare not take off my right kneecap. There are not too many people in this section of the grandstand and most of the standees have already departed on their errands. Of those that are left scattered around me most look unhappy and one or two look happy. Some are winners and most are losers. A few can face the day with an edge and the majority are into the sack and must start behind. I am aware from my marginal contact with what we like to call the "outside world" that this is not an unusual situation in life but it does not make the losing any sweeter or get the fourteen horse up to show some kind of bravery in the deep stretch.

XXVII

STILL-LIFE: HARRY THE FLAT LOSING
ON A DISQUALIFICATION

The horse's number has come up on the board, ten clearly to win and the Flat, patting the moist tickets in his shirt pockets has succumbed, once again, to the illusion that he is omnipotent, that he is on top of the game, that he has within his own hands the means to shape his destiny. But then the *inquiry* light came up, only thirty seconds later or so and now the track announcer has stated that the jockey on the horse which finished fourth has claimed foul against the winner and the stewards will examine the films of the race, do not discard any tickets. A deep thick grunt of rage has come from the crowd at this announcement. The ten horse has been the solid favorite, going off at seven to five or a little bit less and in the bargain this is the second race, the bottom half of the daily double and thousands of students are locked into the favorite for the second race. Thus it is rage, rage and astonishment which seem to filter from the crowd in uneven waves, a haze of emotion so thick that could it be converted to weather on the spot, the track might sink beneath its own purposes and vanish into the surrounding mud. Poised over the rail, his accustomed spot, the Flat has had a few moments of great difficulty in simply assimilating the problem. To contain the single emotion of the accomplishment or loss after a race is difficult enough for him nowadays, now when he must sustain two, balancing them off into something between hope and revulsion. It seems as if the very scatterings and joints of his mind are buckling, the Flat wipes moisture off his forehead with a limp hand, caresses the pages of the program, bends the program over the rail, reaches for and then discards as pointless a cigarette which would only make him inhale upon the foul foretaste of decay, disassembly, death. "Goddamn it," he murmurs which is the best he can do under the circumstances. He has bet fifty win and place on the ten horse and since the objection has come from the horse finishing fourth it means that he cannot even hope for backup money if the horse is disqualified. It will be bumped all the way down to fourth itself while the others scuttle in precedence. He takes out the tickets, looks at them, feels a stab of utter dismay overtake him as he sees that the twenty-five dollars he thought he had bet to place had instead been for show; he must have called the wrong slot to the seller or maybe he is really losing his mind. Not only his mind but his guts, he simply has no stomach for this any more, no sense of control whatsoever, a feeling of large, dim events somehow overtaking him and imploding his life from within. The Flat finds himself wonder if he made a wrong decision many years ago, maybe his father had been right, maybe he should have looked for a trade, something steady that he could do with his hands, no large possibilities in it but no disqualifications either and a union card for the times that it all got too hot. He might have been working in a lumber yard right now or perhaps a metals shop, Harry the Handler, bent over his tools, his face shining with perspiration, intent with involvement, happy in himself and his work because he could see the goddamned results right in front of him and something to come home to at the end of the day too, something that made sense, a wife and a couple of kids and a television set and a few cans of beer too, what the hell, it wasn't much but it beat this. Anything except that goddamned Gertrude who would never shut up and was so full of ideas that if they were turned into parlays little streamers of loss could be ignited over Bensonhurst. Gertrude who was satisfied with absolutely nothing that he did, ever (but then why the hell did she marry him?) and in the bargain was full of small resentments and twitches of her own. Odd long evenings she would spend in the kitchen, drinking coffee and mourning her lost piano lessons, long afternoons on Sunday when he was only trying to squeeze a little percentage out of the *Telegraph* entries and she would ask him, to start a serious discussion, whether he really felt that Bensonhurst was the whole world. There was just no future in it, nothing at all, he had married her for his own reasons and they made sense at the time, they might even make sense now if she would leave him the hell alone but of course that was precisely the one thing that she would never do, leave him alone. If she was able to leave him alone maybe she wouldn't have needed to marry him in the first place, could have done all those things that she said she was about to do but instead it was only a question of Gertrude in the kitchen, Gertrude in the living room, Gertrude every damn place you went and absolutely the same thing in all of them. She would never change her expression or tone of voice, even when she was fucking. She had a good body but what the hell. On balance it simply didn't add up, it didn't figure any more but the kind of backgrounds that they both came from divorce was out of the question, so what was there? What the hell was there? Well, about the only major thing there was was the hope that he could win himself out so big that he could pay her up to and beyond what she thought she deserved, pay her off and the hell with her and then be able to get into the game with some kind of edge. But that was harder and harder all the time, his luck had never been so good in the first place and although he had been able to beat the game in small ways right through the time they had gotten married, everything seemed to have fallen apart since then. His selections weren't working, his timing had fallen apart, he had become superstitious and he had lost his courage as well. Everything was going to pieces, no question about it. The blinking number ten comes off the board at that moment, the crowd muttering and screaming and praying and gets knocked down to fourth position. The announcer says that after their consideration of the films the stewards have found that number ten was guilty of interference on the stretch turn and the objection has been sustained and the revised order of finish is now official. Harry takes out his tickets for the last time, symbolically kisses them, which he has always felt is a pretty gesture, and tears them into colorless shreds, casts them twinkling over the rail. They land in a few puddles of yesterday's slop. Now he feels collapse, a sensation of buildings falling to the right and left of him as he stands on a vacant street somewhere holding out against the wreckers who nevertheless, needle and ball, have moved in to take his life apart. Dwarfish laughter in the skies, terrific power in the rolling concrete, flickering and incision of light behind him as he turns to run but there is nowhere to run, they are demolishing the whole fucking city it now turns out and so Harry the Flat stands as best he can against all these difficulties, man holding out against his destiny, reading the one remaining copy of the *Morning Telegraph* which they have kindly lent him to provide illustrations for his prescience. At length someone in the sky says that in the third race the number three, Royal Red, is four pounds over and he hastens to make the alteration on his program, knocking out the three who is going from nowhere, strictly from nowhere, underneath all that weight.

XXVIII

AN EXEGESIS OF BILLY CHART

There has been dispute for some time as to the true nature and function of Billy Chart: whether he merely figures out the races for the top connections and gives them an experienced opinion supplemented by research, computation, intuition and the kind of academic knowhow which can only be provided by a college degree in mathematics . . . or whether, as some have proposed, he is not predicting the races but actually manipulating them, giving over to the top connections every evening his planned program of intent for the next day. If the latter is true then the Chart is absolutely diabolical. He is able to muddle in his head not only the records and potential of several hundred horses but is able to decide exactly in which fashion their histories should be recorded, the timing of wins, losses, run-ins, disqualifications, and so on. It is because this second task seems to me to be utterly out of range of man or demon that I have opted for the point of view that the Chart is merely a brilliant handicapper but every now and then, when particularly insane things happen at this track of my choice, I am not so sure. In either case, the likelihood of definite word is quite slight; the Chart will talk business to no one and after an evening's effort will go only to Tony Winner in whose backroom premises he is often known to be locked up for several hours, discussing, no doubt, the nature of the weather at Aqueduct and his reminiscences of his college days and so on.

The Chart is visible at most times if one knows where to look; he does most of his work at Pop Warner's and now and then, on weekends, at the Little Invalid. His appearance is so characteristic, not to say distinctive, that it is impossible to mistake him for anyone else. He is also, as the saying goes, a reasonably accessible man in that he is willing to put down his charts and memoirs at almost any given time to talk with someone he knows. The only problem is that he will discuss absolutely anything except the horses. On the horses he has absolutely no comment and those who have attempted to break this policy with strong drink or threats have found that the Chart, under pressures of this sort, is apt to become ugly and full of false information . . . and that the Winner, the next day, is apt to become even uglier. It simply does not pay then to become too closely involved with the Chart although he is a fascinating man and in other circumstances, say at a college of higher learning, might be well-received and highly-respected for his articulate nature and his rather liberal points of view on contemporary subjects of particular interest. "This country is absolutely post-technologized but what the social scientists do not understand is that the post-technological era began way back, began in 1900 as a matter of fact and that what we took to be the beginning of the industrial revolution was in sociological terms really its end. The whole life-style which we thought of as technologized really is a reaction to it," is a characteristic statement of the well-spoken Chart and although there is no one in or around the vicinity of Pop Warner's capable of discussing the point with him at his serious level there is no question but that the Chart makes a good argument for himself and that almost anything he says is likely to be of great interest.

It is of great interest from the scientific point of view at any rate, although the woods and prisons are filled with men who tried to piece together from the Chart's conversation hints on the next day's selections and horses to watch and so on and so forth. These unfortunate horseplayers, perhaps being more adapted than I to the theory that the world is essentially a benign and meaningful territory to occupy, theorized that the Chart was under Tony Winner's thumb but carried around at all times the desire to do fellow workers of the turf well, and tried to do this in various oblique ways for which all of his academic discussions were merely a cover. Thus when the Chart would say, "we're in an age of declining consumption I would think; per capita consumption has actually gone down within the last twenty years because there's simply an insufficiency of goods which you can convince the urbanized they really desire. As far as the disadvantaged, there are simply more and more of them fighting for the same amount which is disproportionate not to say reduced," some unfortunate punter might get the idea that what the Chart was actually pointing out was that Per Capita, the roan filly in tomorrow's fifth, looked like a spot at the odds or that Insufficiency, the bay plater in the starter handicap might be a very good bet. Many serious horseplayers came to grief because of their speculations on the philosophy of Billy Chart but since it was well known in and out of the trade that Billy Chart's health and well being was under the paternal aegis of Tony Winner, it was felt injudicious for any of the losers to point out to him the difficulties involved by being a serious student of the Chart's metaphysics.

I could have pointed out to any of them (but of course did not, having my own troubles, not to say complexities of the inner life) that it was almost hopeless to deduce tips from the Chart because he was sincerely and passionately dedicated to his intellectual theories when not on the figures and obtained genuine pleasure from the use of his mind as entirely apart from the company it produced. Beyond that and more importantly, the nature of modern racing and breeders' naming is such that on any given card there were apt to be at least three or four horses whose names had been bounded into the Chart's lectures and these horses could be assumed to be connected to the Chart inasmuch as he had studied their background and had, perhaps, subconsciously, incorporated them into his essays of the higher life. It is, in any event, a point of fact that Utica and Troy, New York are filled with plumbers, bricklayers and mortician's assistants who at one time in their earlier years felt that the path to revelation lay straight through Billy Chart's philosophical studies and spent many weeks or months at his feet trying to gather the word from him.

Because Billy Chart is known for his linguistics, his computations and his overall quietude about the matter of his employment, his intercepting me on my way from the Winner's studio after my dialogue last night was particularly surprising and what transpired after that is complex enough to lend something of an overage to the tasks which I must perform today. Chart took me by the elbow as I was midway poised between the bar and door and the street and escorted me quietly to an upper level of the bar to the rear, his glasses glinting in his characteristic scholarly fashion. His intelligent face had a certain pallor, reminding me once again, if I ever needed reminding, that the Chart is a serious man and that serious consequences await anyone who does not see him in that light. "It is important that I talk to you," he said, passing his drink over the bar to me, "the Winner is very, very upset about certain things and I must advise you of the urgency. Finish my drink, I don't want it. I was only drinking to pass the time away until you emerged. Actually, despite the fact that half my life seems to be spent in saloons, I am really not a serious drinker."

I tasted the drink which appeared to be one of those deadly sugared concoctions which, when I was younger, had caused me so much difficulty and said, "I'm not quite sure what the problem is." Caution was the watchword of the time, the Chart, as I hope I have suggested is, perhaps, not to be trifled with and in the bargain I was shaken by my conversation with the Winner who I did not need to be told was extremely serious. "Would you care to tell me?"

"You're doing the job, aren't you? I mean, that's what he arranged with you, right? I mean, I couldn't stand it if after he promised and promised he wasn't doing it."

"All right," I said, finishing off the drink in a single horrid gulp, feeling it recede within me, as my fond memories for Harry the Flat had somehow passed away before my eyes, when I became involved with his widow, "there is no reason to be concerned. I have been detailed to do an excavation."

"Ah," the Chart said, keeling over the bar with a groan of relief and then raising one of his thin and deft hands to curl hair away from his forehead as if he were handling a pencil, "ah, that is very good to hear. You must do this. It must be done quickly."

"I am doing it tomorrow."

"You don't understand," the Chart said, "no one understands except me and I don't know if I made it clear to them back there at all. The whole thing is falling to pieces. I can't make the computations anymore. It's all screwed up due to that stiff. Nothing works."

"So I have been advised."

"It's out of control. The whole thing is that it's out of control and I can't get my hands on it anymore. Listen, there was a time up until very recently when the sprints were being affected but I always knew that I would be able to work out a mile or a mile and an eighth race because in the routes, class tends to stand up and they can come back from being knocked off stride and do what they have to. So you could lay off the sprints and still make the figure but the point is it's gotten so bad that nothing works. Not even the mile and a half stuff which they run occasionally over the main course. The conditions are so bad that they don't ever seem to come back. It don't affect the turf races of course, the turf races are still all right on the inner grass courses but how many turf races are there a day? and anyway the factors don't stand up too well there for other reasons. I don't know. I just don't know what to say. The whole thing could drive you crazy; they got to get hold of it."

This was the first time that I had ever found Billy Chart in the actual act of discussing horse-racing and it was this more than anything else that made me tremble. Not the cast of his face or the movement of his hands but the fact that the Chart would actually get into the subject of horses filled me with a distinct and unpleasant ominousness which made all the difficulties with the Winner pass away as if in an inner breeze. I ordered a martini, which is a very unusual gesture for me, and then ordered one for the Chart—whose rate of respiration and internal movement seemed to be on the increase. "Be calm," I said to him, passing down an excellent wooden dish of nuts, "be calm, everything will be taken care of in the long run." This advice sounded strange coming from me but on the other hand the whole conversation was very strange. When the drink was put in front of the Chart he knocked it off in one swallow as if it were beer and then, wiping his lips, turned to me and jolted the nuts onto the floor. "Leave them," the bartender said from down a distance, "just leave them. Let them scramble for it; they'll think it's selections."

"I used to be an alcoholic," the Chart said, "in fact, I had a very promising career as an alcoholic until I got sidetracked into a mathematics degree by virtue of the GI Bill of Rights, which is an actual swindle. You see, the thing is that I think I'm losing control. It was nice for a while, you could move them in and out, up and down in class, work out things the way they appealed to you. There were limits, of course, and actually you were kind of tightly controlled, like being sure to make the favorites win one out of every three races and be in the money two out of every three times. They are very strict about that and there are also tight percentages for second favorites and longshots and like that. Actually, you'd be surprised how little freedom you have in the job. But every year you could do one or two things really interesting and creative; you could take a liking to a thirty-five hundred dollar gelding, for instance, just on his name or looks and you'd work him into a couple of races and move him right up in class and maybe by the end of the year he'd be running for twenty five thousand or even in allowances. That would always keep things interesting and the prices were good too. Or you could work it the other way; there would be a stakes gelding, for instance, who you didn't care for and maybe you had something against the trainer and they got to listen to you so you'd start to drop him down and down and by September *he'd* be running for thirty five hundred. You know what I always liked to do the most? You know what the most fun was? You would take one of these and drop him down and down and finally he'd end up in a thirty five hundred dollar race which you knew they couldn't stand. What I liked was to have him win galloping and then he'd get claimed away from them and start moving up in class. Oh, I loved that! But it's all gone to hell the past year; I can't stand it anymore. Could I have another drink?"

I passed him over my martini, feeling very sober and in possession of my faculties for possibly the first time that day and extracted a cigarette, trying to light it calmly and preserve the tenor of the discussion. "Look," I said, "look, do I gather right? Is it the truth? You're the one who arranges all the races and makes the results come out. You mean you're setting the whole thing up?"

"They won't let me bet," the Chart said, working on the second martini as if it were the solution to the first. "They won't let me bet, they're very strict about that kind of thing, the betting has to be tightly controlled and if they ever discovered me doing any betting, even through a cover-up, it would be very bad. They pay me two hundred dollars a week and my expenses. Two hundred dollars isn't all the money in the world but you'd be surprised—" and he stopped dead at exactly that moment because Tony Winner, looking very determined, emerged from his office, turned toward the bar, saw us there and came toward the Chart meaningfully, his hands gripping and ungripping. Behind him, two of his associates, who I had but rarely glimpsed before, looked at us with unusual intentness, then went to the door and leaned their shoulders against it convincingly. In all the books and papers I have read about the Mob, this kind of action indicates that serious trouble is brewing but as it so turned out I was so numbed by the Chart's series of inferences, to say nothing of the martini atop the Winner's instructions, that it all failed to connect. "You people having a companionable drink together?" the Winner said, stepping between us. I should have pointed out somewhere along the way that the Winner is a very small and strongly built man, five foot six or so but well over one hundred and fifty pounds and exceedingly menacing in appearance with a face and head that seemed to have been transplanted from a man much taller. Also he had massive shoulders and all in all, even without the question of the associates, one would not want to get into a serious difference of opinion with the Winner. "I thought that you were told to go home."

"No," I said, "you didn't say that. Not that I ain't. Not that I wasn't going to head home this minute. It was just the Chart. The Chart invited me to share a drink and I felt it sheerly propitious—"

"Don't look at me," the Chart said in a high whine, raising his hands and backing away from the bar, "it had nothing to do with me, he just wanted to share a drink. Anyway I was just heading back home. Look, I am not even married, I have no wife and children, I can not even claim pre-marital associations. You are not dealing with a man who has very much. I can't even handle liquor too well. Show some sympathy, some understanding."

"You have a loose head," the Winner said. "An extremely loose and disjointed head and there appears to be no dealing with you."

"But you don't understand, we were merely talking about social dislocation and cultural dysfunction in the post-technological, secular society, chief. That's all and then he started to get argumentative—"

"I think we will give you an escort," the Winner said. "That is to say, I think that we will help you get home, inasmuch as you seem to be having some difficulties on your own making that journey."

"Well, all right," the Chart said rather trepidatiously and ran a hand over the bar, "if you insist, that is all right, but I do not think—"

"It is highly necessary," Tony Winner said, "and I will, with one of my companions, perform that duty. The other companion will take you home," he said to me, "since you seem to be having concurrent difficulties."

"I'll do it," I said rather pointlessly. "Believe me, I'll do it. This mission to me is not only a job but an act of a sacrifice, a penance for an old dear friend. Nothing in the world would give me more true pleasure than to perform this act well and to—"

"Of course you'll perform it," the Winner said, "you will perform everything because you are one of these people made to follow orders but I do not discard the possibility of a little education after the fact." He motioned his companions over; dropping their shoulders, looking with some loathing at the Chart, they joined us. "William and I," the Winner said, "are going to afford the Chart a drive home. David, you will take this gentleman here to his destination. Is that clearly understood?"

"That's all right," the one called David said. Close up, from a view I had never inspected before, he seemed to be a somewhat enlarged and fuzzier version of the Winner but in a dim light this would be no help. "I would be pleased to escort this man home." He put his hand on my shoulder, creating a definite and unpleasant pressure to which I submitted, having learned at a different period of my life (but one no less important) that submission at certain times is the best of all possible worlds or at least not the worst.

"Just home, David," the Winner said. "I appreciate your enthusiasm and dedication to our point and purpose but there is no need to take further action at that time. The man is to be taken home pleasantly, swiftly and courteously."

"Oh, that's all right," David said, "I wouldn't think of doing nothing else any wise. I'm not one of those sadists."

"Cultural inferences," the Chart said, "and the slow dislocation of time. We will continue our discussion at some later interval and I will be able to fill you in on the quantum theory."

"Quantum Theory," the Winner murmured and with the help of his associate took the Chart out of the bar. David and I followed at a respectable distance, his arm almost lovingly around my shoulders. "I have an excellent air-conditioned 1971 Impala," he said, "which premises I am sure you will enjoy. There is no need not to relax with me, everything, as you know, will be all right."

"Fine," I said, making no effort to escape the grasp, "that's fine."

"You're the guy who is supposed to be doing the job tomorrow, is that right?"

"I'm the man."

"How does the bomb feel?"

"I don't feel anything," I said. "It's just kind of a pressure in the thigh. It went in very quick and they closed it right up. You'd hardly know it except if you bump yourself which I do not intend to do in any way whatsoever."

"It isn't, uh, sexual or anything like that, is it?"

"Huh?"

"The bomb. In your thigh. I mean, it don't give you sexual feelings."

"It's nowhere near there," I assured him, "nowhere near that part at all," and we continued in silence to his car; in the car he put the air-conditioning and stereo on and loosened up quite considerably, even to the point of advising me how badly the Chart had been suffering in these recent weeks, how badly all of them had been suffering under the surprising and unfortunate circumstances and how grateful he, speaking personally, was that the condition was being rectified. Imbued with too much information already that evening I kept a respectful silence all the way home, not even taking the bait from him when he began to curse Billy Chart who, he said, he believed to be somehow involved in the problems himself and might have lost his touch or his connections and was only blaming the stiff to take a little of the heat off his own directions. "I don't know," I said, "it's all too complicated for me, I never went to college," and we went home and he escorted me out in a lover's embrace, into the vestibule of my two-family in Bensonhurst. A long, firm, careful gaze followed me up the stairs away from him as if I were a woman he was trying to promote, but only in the most inferential way.

I listened for his car to drive away which it did not, expectedly, for a very long time, but finally it did and then I tried to make myself as comfortable as possible in the circumstances of the time bomb and the anticipation, trying to lie on the other side, trying not to think of George Needles' handiwork. But as I tried to sleep and then to dream, all that I could see were pictures of the Chart: the Chart was in the infield lake at Aqueduct, huddled with the swans and he was drowning, drowning naked in the pond. "Help, help!" the Chart screamed but could not attract sufficient attention to his plight because a race was in progress and the crowd otherwise occupied, the noise volume high, the attention fixated elsewhere. "Help, help!" the Chart screamed again and went belly-up in the pond, swans coming then to pick at his tiny genitalia as the horses stumbled by toward the wire, the fluttering of swan's wings concealing from the preoccupied crowd the picture of this deeper and more significant swindle.

XXIX

HOW HARRY THE FLAT'S TIP-SHEET
SCHEME IN AUGUST OF 1960
FINALLY WORKED OUT

To his random mailing of one hundred appeals, the Flat received fourteen answers, one from an account executive in metals and one from a promising young starlet who even he had heard of. The replies all came into his post office box within two days of one another and when it became apparent that it would come to no more, the Flat sat down in his apartment, surrounded by his single friend and associate and fanning them out on a table said, "now you have to look for an angle. Two hundred and ten is hardly worth the trouble of going into it unless you find an angle."

"Two hundred and ten dollars provides the expenses and makes it worth your while," the associate pointed out and the Flat said, "that is quite true but now I am in the awful position of having to give out a winner and I am not quite sure what would be the best way of doing this. In the meantime, I must do some thinking," and took the proceeds down to Winner stating that this was a good faith payment and indicated that the Flat was trying to meet his responsibilities and would, and thus only needed a little more time. The Winner said that he would think about this and the Flat returned, the whole visit having taken only three minutes, since at that time, due to certain extrinsic influences, he had rented rooms right above the Winner's then habitat. "I know what I'll do," he said as if the conversation had never been interrupted, "I'll scatter fourteen longshots through the nine races and give each of them out to one. I ought to hit at least two or three of them and the five dollar win bets will give me enough finance to go into this in a bigger way. In addition to that, those who win will love and trust and depend upon me and I will find it much easier to raise their ante in the future." The Flat then took out the entries for the following day's races and hastily made some notes. "The calls will all be coming in at the same time," he noted, "I will have to arrange with Sally so that she doesn't object to the booth being tied up for a while."

The Flat then proceeded to pick fourteen horses in the nine races, all of whose odds were upwards of twenty to one in the morning line while his friend and associate comported himself with drinks, confidences and that other regalia of friendship which had been his due with the Flat for some time. It was not so much that the friend and associate was in awe of the Flat as that he felt the perverse desire to protect, which sometimes came over him also when he looked at apprentice jockeys. The Flat, oblivious of all those significances did his work and went to sleep with a justified smile on his benevolent (in that aspect) face.

Unfortunately, the scheme did not work out so good. In the first place, the Flat by this system was able to locate no less than five winners on this day of longshots, handed out to the various people, and in the second place not one of them found it fit or necessary to pay the proceeds of a five dollar win bet. The prices on the five winners were $59.20, $86.40, $32.70, $114.50 and $49.10 and a ten dollar win bet on even the smallest of them would have been worth eighty dollars to the Flat, leaving out of the question the nearly three hundred that would have been returned on the largest and leaving entirely to one side the issue of parlays which the Flat might have considered.

"People," the Flat said a week later when it became apparent that his correspondents had vanished into the same place where yesterday's Top Turf letters do, "fucking people. They got no honesty. They got no respect. They are nothing but a bunch of dishonest charlatans and that will be my final evaluation after all these years of living."

Much later, in somewhat different circumstances, the Flat tried the approach again but it drew no responses and as it turned out the horse that he genuinely intended to tip on was scratched out and shipped permanently to Dover Downs. More direct means, from then on in, appealed to him.

XXX

BEFORE THE SECOND, A SURPRISING INTERVENTION: A SCENT LIKE GAS MEANWHILE DRIFTS FROM THE INFIELD TOTE

Fifteen dollars, therefore in the hole. Locked into that curious insulation which takes over any serious horseplayer before a race, I am examining the *Telegraph* carefully, deciding what would be the most propitious horse on which to lose money in the second, when I am startled by a tap on the shoulder. My first thought is that it is one of the Winner's assistants come to check on my presence and the second, even more difficult to assimilate, is that it might be George Needles's time bomb which, due to certain mechanical defects, is making its presence known some ten hours too early but when I turn I find myself confronted instead by a small, dignified, grey man adorned by a goatee and a set of random jewels which infest various parts of the jacket he wears. The jacket is also grey (I should mention that so are the pants) and the jewels, being of many different colors, lend a certain cheerful relief to his appearance although not, unfortunately, enough to entirely relieve me. "Pardon me," he says, noting the cello case and my program with one judicious sweep of his eyes, "you are the man I believe I was meant to see. Won't you come along with me, please?"

"I don't believe I understand you," I say, my normal racetrack surliness being compounded by all kinds of circumstances, "I'm not seeing anyone."

"Oh come on, my friend, don't be ridiculous. We don't have the time. I was advised to locate a man in the upper grandstand with a cello case and a certain expression around the eyes and you have both. Will you come with me? There are certain matters that must be discussed."

I put the *Telegraph* down in as circumspect a way as possible and say, "if there's anything to discuss it can be settled right up here. I'm rather busy and I don't have any winners."

"Oh yes you do," he says rather vaguely and tips his head, regarding the tote. "You know something?" he says in rather confidential fashion, "I really hate the races. I don't understand them and I don't know what's going on. How people can get involved in something like this, throw their money away is beyond me. The whole thing sickens me."

The circumstances of being locked deep into some kind of defensive discussion with a grey little man in goatee and jewels thrusts me, perhaps, deeper into surliness than I have been for a while and I say, "listen, friend, I told you, I'm very busy. I got a lot of things to do up here. Why don't you just leave me alone? You want a contribution for something, I have a few cents."

"Oh come off that," he says in a harsher tone. "Stop that nonsense, we have no time for it. I told you, a discussion is in order."

"So discuss it up here. You have anything to say? I'm listening."

"You don't understand. It's not me, I am merely a messenger. I have been detailed to contact you and bring you to the appropriate place. On my own, I have nothing to discuss. I don't even understand the races. How could anyone?"

"That's it, buddy," I say and stand to my full height which although only five feet ten is relatively somewhat impressive at the racetrack which is generally filled with shorter men. "I want to hear no more of this starting right now."

"Don't be an ass," he whispers to me with an unusual and flowing sibilance, bending his little lips back so that his teeth, grey and pearly, fairly glisten in the clouds, "do you think you're really going to get out of this alive? You're the only definite witness they got to the whole thing, the only one who can spill the business and you got a time bomb in you set for midnight which will conveniently remove you from the picture. You think they're really going to take that thing out? Like hell they are; I bet you six to five that they don't even have a removal device *on* that thing, it just goes off."

"You said you didn't know nothing about odds," I say rather weakly but it is merely a weak complaint, not attuned to the general situation whatsoever and I find myself staggering, the very air seeming to dissolve and stagnate around me, impression of birds fluttering in the heat and I sit down abruptly, feeling a dangerous pressure around my inner thigh which instantly reminds me not to be abrupt. Somehow it seems difficult to pull myself into momentary accord with the situation. "How'd you know?" I find myself saying, "how'd you know anyway? The whole thing was supposed to be being kept under wraps. I had it promised—"

"Come now," he says, taking me tenderly by an upper elbow and helping me to my feet again with far more vigor than might be expected from such a delicately-chiseled man, "come now, don't be ridiculous about this again. Did you really think that som ₋ng like this could be kept under cover? Everybody knows, believe me. We only want to help, to discuss this whole thing reasonably. There are things you ought to know, we feel you're entitled. Or I should say *they* feel; I'm not really involved in this being a messenger of sorts. There now, isn't that better? Come along," and so I do come along, reaching my free hand to take the cello case which I balance uneasily and permit myself to be led down the steps and up the ramp and through the door and then to the escalator. Having accomplished his mission, the little man seems to have detached himself completely, only the hand retaining connection, otherwise he shakes his head, mutters something, checks his watch against the tote and escorts me tenderly.

It is a strange sensation being conducted through the maze of Aqueduct by a small, neatly-constructed little man while carrying a cello case; I feel as if I were a musician being led to an important date by the conductor or perhaps a cello repairman being taken by the cellist to the home of his condition, all of this detachment and fantasy heightened by the density of the escalators, the noise of horseplayers, the blaring of the announcer. I had never realized until this time how noisy the racetrack was, having been so much more involved in my own self-excursions, but now I see that it is, perhaps, the noisiest place available in all western society outside of a construction site and I try to visualize in compensation an orchestra playing quietly, the *Swan Lake* possibly, or maybe one of the Boccherini cello concertos, anything to detach me from Aqueduct. Obviously, it is too late to entertain ambitions of this sort and in addition, my thigh, aided by the bump, is beginning to itch dreadfully. I want to put my fingers into the spot and dig and scratch, but obviously think better of this kind of impulse. At length we come to the first floor of the grandstand and my escort leads me toward the rear, the cashier's window section and finally to a Harry M. Stevens cigarettes & candy concession station, station number 161 as a matter of fact, where a large blonde woman behind the counter sights me and smiles and then takes me from the grasp of the grey man as tenderly as any woman has ever touched me. "Hello there," she says, "I'm so glad you came. You got him then with no trouble?"

"No trouble at all. I had to shock him a little bit I'm afraid, but that's all."

"Well I can see you shocked him a little bit, you look just terrible honey. Why don't you sit down?", she says and pulls a stool from the side, pushes me gently down into it, removes the cello case from my limp fingers and puts it to one side. "That's fine, Gerry," she says, "that's just great. You can go ahead and take care of your business now."

"Do you want me to hang around?"

"It's up to you."

"I really hate the racetrack, Julie. If it's all the same to you, I'd really rather get out."

"Well that's fine, hon, you just go ahead and do anything you want to do because now we've got the man of the hour here," she says and allows her fingers to dribble across my forehead, coolness against the damp, a scent of gas wafting in from the inner tote and causes my body to contract and then yelp with sweat. "Everything's great," she says and the grey man nods, pokes me gently in the unimplanted thigh and leaves. "He's all right," she says. "He doesn't understand the horses but he's efficient and he has a very gentle streak."

"I didn't even bet the second," I say, "listen, I'd better go and bet the second—"

"Oh sweetheart," she says tenderly and produces another stool, seats her-

self next to me, puts up a sign on the counter saying OUT OF ORDER so
that two customers tapping the counter shrug and prepare to look for their
outlets elsewhere, "oh, sweetheart, it's too late for any of this now. Please don't
be coy; it isn't fair to anyone and it doesn't become you. Let's talk very directly."

"But who are you?" I say. "I mean, I've never patronized this stand before.
Usually I buy my cigarettes and other stuff before I get here; the charges are
just too much so I don't know anyone."

"Lots of guys feel that way," she says, "this is just such a cheap company
that they squeeze every nickel, they don't understand that they'd do ten
times the business if they gave the consumer a break but you see the way they
figure it is that the turnover at the racetrack is so quick all the time that they
might as well get them while they're here because next time they won't be.
This is my theory anyway."

"That's very interesting."

"I try to think a lot about these things when I have the time," the woman
called Julie says, "but we really don't have the time; I have to make this very
fast. You know why you came down here, didn't you? I mean, I don't have to
start from the top, do I? he told you everything."

"He didn't tell me nothing," I say as two more customers, released like birds
from the coop of the crowd come over fluttering to look for cigarettes, see the
intensity of our conversation and mumbling walk away, holding one another's arms. "I don't know nothing at all but it looks like business—" and
at that point the cello case which I have been supporting on my lap falls to the
floor with a horrid clunk, rolls painfully on my instep and settles, quiescent.
I look, fascinated, to see if the implements will once again follow but they do
not and the remainder of my attention is diverted by a hand on my knee:
clamping, viselike, but with a distant warmth that might under different circumstances even excite me, as horrid a thought as this must be. "Oh Lord,"
she says, "I thought you had been filled in; I mean I figured that they had had
the decency to at least tell you what you were doing out here. But then again
why should they? that's the way they operate, in absolute contempt for people. I see then I'm going to have to take it from the top. I have to do this quick
you understand because we just don't have the time but if you listen to me for
just a minute or so I can fill you in and then you'll understand. You a bright
guy? You see, the thing is that you have to grasp all of this fast."

"I don't know," I say, "I wasn't figured for bright, which is maybe why I
ended up here."

"That's true of all of them," she says, "but it ain't brains missing, it's just
organization. Listen to me now. Listen intent and listen quick and I will give
you the total smarts on the situation here and make you understand what has
been done to you."

"I wish I could lay something down on the second," I say wishfully, deterred by the grasp on my knee from any more definite reaction. "It's just an old policy, I never missed a bet."

"Forget it," she says, leaning forward and fixing me with her cool, storming gaze which like her grasp, locks in and hints at depths far beyond the rather simpleminded nature of her occupation and Harry M. Stevens concession hat, "forget it, I can always tell by looking at the way the Adam's apple in the neck moves. Although there's nothing personal in this, you understand, and you got to look at it only as a scientific explanation, the fact is that you're a loser. A loser, my friend. A loser now and in the future and you got to begin to deal in accordance with that fact.

"Now hear me out."

XXXI

WHAT JULIE TOLD ME

Now the first thing you got to understand is that this Mob of yours, which
like all the simpleminded people you associate with, you take to be the end
and center of all existence, is only part of the question. There is a Mob, of
course, and that's not to be denied, but they control only half of the situation.
The other half is controlled by an organization which is set up in about the
same way but for exactly the opposite purposes, antithetical to it in every way,
to use the kind of word I rarely do and hate to but find it fits the present circumstances. We might as well call this other organization 'the Counters' just
to give you a convenient tag to call it because I know that you don't make it
very well with abstractions. Gerry and I happen to be members of this organization, not very high of course, make it in the middle-levels, roughly
where the Winner is with the Mob.

Now the thing is with your Mob that they've moved up in the world,
they've been around for a long time and for most of it were a kind of small-
time organization without luck or skill, just hanging around on the fringes.
Post-technology, which came along in 1900, pretty well knocked them out of
the box even though they had been around for a hundred years before that because they just weren't able to deal with the post-technological devices too
good, they weren't set up for it. So they just kind of moved along on the un-
derside for a long, long time, picking up the fringe energy and hustling off the
margins. It's pretty safe to say that the whole arrangement was being run by
the Counters who were a newer, smaller, more adventurous organization back
in the nineteen hundreds and were able to see the way the drift was going and
were able to make adjustments. But the Mob fell into a kind of luck after its
long wasteland and period in the desert. In about 1963, late 1963, they were
able to get hold of the situation and from then right up until a few months ago
they were pretty well running things themselves. It was quite a reversal as you
can expect and the fact that the whole world seems to have turned around in
these eight years is because of the change of direction, but I really can't get too
technical about this because it would take too much time and you wouldn't
be able to grasp it. Even I'm not able to grasp it: it takes a lifetime of study and
preparation at the highest levels to grasp the reasons and there's no time for
them at the bottom.

But as best as we can figure out it was at the time Kennedy was assassinated,
whether or not they were actually responsible for it or whether they simply
saw an edge, a way to move into a difficult situation and fake it out we aren't
quite clear yet. Certainly, this can be admitted: the Counters had been running things for a long, long time and the organization had gotten kind of

frozen; back in 1963 there was a lot of dead wood at top levels which maybe was on the way to being eased out and maybe not but it was ripe for some kind of takeover. Most of the theories do hold that the Mob was able to maneuver the assassination and then slip in right quickly to take advantage but that's only discussion and it doesn't matter. In any event, it's been their ballgame for seven years now and I admit that they've given the Counters a run for their money. On the other hand, there was a big shakeup in the Counter organization right after the assassination when new blood moved up and a lot of realistic people took over the situation. Certainly if those people had been around at the time this never would have happened. But by then it was too late.

So the thing is that they got hold of the situation, opportunism or luck and they've been calling the shots now for a while. They've been running the races and the other stuff pretty much as they wanted to but you see what happened, when your friend the Flat had that accident back in 1967, even though they didn't know it, that was the beginning of the end for them. It took a long time for the excavation to begin to penetrate to the actual soil of the backstretch but as close as we can figure it they lost the ability to get hold of the races a couple of months ago. Their figures have been knocked all to pieces and they just can't control the races anymore. And if they can't control the races, you see, they can't run the world. It all runs in a straight line from the races right through everything else but the races come first. If they lose the ability to maneuver those, then that's it.

Now I understand that this is kind of a hard thing to grasp, how being able to control the races would mean that you'd be able to get hold of every single other thing in the world and if that's an explanation you want, I'm afraid that I won't be able to help you very much. I studied very little of it myself. Everybody in the Counters gets a full survey course in which you learn the history and background and elements. I picked up a few things but it was only a couple weeks course many years ago and even then I wasn't sure what they were talking about. The fact that the Counters, at least, try to teach the people working for them why the system is that way and how they work means that they're a better organization right off the top than your Mob, which can only move through fear—but I just throw that in as a selling point. The fact is that I'm not one of the theoreticians, I'm just more of a lookout, an observer you might say, used in this Harry M. Stevens concession location so that I can keep a lookout on the races which are central to almost everything else. More or less I'm a reporter and investigator although now and again as you see I'm licensed to do contact work.

Now the fact is that we know exactly what's going on with the Mob, we know exactly what they're up to and it came to our awareness just as soon as it did to theirs, that the only way they could regain control of the races was to get your friend's body out of that backstretch. Then it was a matter of simplicity to find out when and how they were going to do it and who was involved and so on and their methods. So we've had our eye on this all along and that's why I'm able to speak to you now.

So you see, the whole thing is very simple when you come right down to it. If you dig your friend out of the backstretch like they hired you to do, then the backstretch will be all right again and the figures will work and they'll be able to handle the races again because we just took over and frankly we're not very strong and we've had the upper hand for so little time really that we just couldn't resist their strength once they got back into control again. And then things would pick up just the way they have been since the Mob took over: the atrocities and the riots and the rigged races and the wrong speed ratings and the suffering and dislocation and so on. Just if you take care of the backstretch job.

On the other hand, if we can persuade you not to do it, then the figures will still be loused up, they won't be able to make the charts stand up, the races will continue to get away from them and we'll be able to reassert our control. We'll be able in a year or even less, just granted a little head start to run the thing all over again just like we did before. And tell me, wouldn't that be better?

Wouldn't you rather have peace and justice and good prices and formful ratings than what you been putting up with the last seven years? Wouldn't it be nice if things went back to the way they used to be and life made sense again? The Counters have always operated by trying to make sense of the world; the Mob is so bizarre and greedy that they don't care. Don't you remember how things used to be? Don't you remember how it was when you could live your life as if it mattered and could make a difference and wasn't being fought over by fifteen hundred bastards? When you could work out speed ratings and consistency charts and they mattered? They could be that way again. Nothing's changed in the world; it's still the same spot that it was a long time ago. Only the management changed but now we got a chance, for the first time since the Kennedy business, to change the management. Wouldn't that be better? Wouldn't you rather have it that way?

So it's up to you. Only you can make the decision. If you follow through on what the Winner instructed you to do we'll go right back to where we were before and things may not change for fifty years . . . and the way your Mob is running things, in fifty years they'll have finished off the whole thing because they're so damned incompetent. On the other hand, if you have the bravery and strength to resist and to stand up against the Mob and tell them that you won't rescue the Flat, then the Mob can't save the races, they'll lose control of things and things will pass to us. Things will get better, finally. The planet will have a second chance and wouldn't that be nice?

So I don't want to overemphasize the urgency or sound melodramatic or anything like that at all because the Counters try to believe in justice and decency and temperance but we might as well lay it straight on the line because it's called for, and say that the whole fate of the world is up to you. It's on your shoulders and only you can make that decision. It's kind of a big thing to ask of a man but if you think of what's best for the whole of mankind rather than for yourself or the Mob you'll see that there's only one thing to do and I know you'll leave him there. You'll leave the ashes in heat and ice, leave him filtering slowly to silt in the darkness so that once again a little bit of beauty and reason can return to this tortured world. I get all carried away when I think about it.

No sir this booth is closed, I'm not selling any cigarettes until at least the fourth. You can pick them up the next booth down by the escalator or you can ride the escalator to the third level and meet this very nice lady named Margaret who will take care of any of your needs.

XXXII

THE QUESTION OF CONSCRIPTION.
A SURPRISE IN THE SECOND

"It's all too much," I say, when I have absorbed this as well as I think I am ever going to be able to absorb the matter. "It's too much for me. I don't think I understand any of it. Counters. Mob. The Flat. Besides, the whole thing's improbable. It's insane. You must think I'm stupid."

"I had to give it to you fast, sweetheart," she says. I should point out that through all of this her clamp upon my knee has not relaxed and the knee now feels absolutely bloodless. Slowly I move it away from her cupped palm, and perhaps trusting me to be immobile now she relaxes the grasp and pats her hair into place. She looks exactly like a Stevens concession lady; flighty, tired, a crinkle of malice around the eyes. It is hard to accept that she is not your everyday Stevens lady. Perhaps she *is* your everyday Stevens lady. The kind of job she holds could make anyone unstable. On the other hand, there is nothing particularly sane about the condition of Harry the Flat or Billy Chart's suggestion of the evening previous. "I don't know," I say. "I just don't know."

"I can't explain it again."

"Listen lady," I say, finally allowing a little bit of my personality ooze forth and it is a pleasure, after the constant oppression of the last days or months (it is hard to distinguish which) to finally assert myself, to suspect that there is something inside still worth asserting, "listen lady, I'm not entirely stupid, even though this cello case and the time bomb might give you the wrong ideas. Accepting everything you say, which I don't, because I think that the Mob is only one organization, not two, accepting all of that, why are you talking to me? Why are you appealing? An organization like the one you describe—"

"The Counters," she says.

"Well, yeah, the Counters, whatever you call yourselves, an organization that you say ruled the world and wants to rule it again, well why are you talking to me. Why don't you simply make sure that I'm not around at the beginning of the eighth to do the job and that would solve the whole problem? It just doesn't make sense."

"It wouldn't, you poor chicken," she says and hands me a pack of Philip Morris filter king cigarettes, courtesy of the house apparently, helps me unwrap the cellophane tenderly and then puts one into my lips and lights it almost lovingly, "it wouldn't because you don't understand the way the Counters work or what kind of organization they are. All your life you've been deep into your Mob where the only means of doing things are violence and coercion and you can understand nothing else. You're so used to being beaten by them that they've made it all you understand. We don't work that way you see. We can't. The Counters aren't that kind of organization and never were."

"I don't get it," I say, puffing on the filter king which seems to have a rather ratty taste; a hint of filly dung in it or possibly the sweat of a maiden gelding. I do not smoke often enough to make informed criticism so keep quiet about this. "I just don't understand."

"Well, then you won't. The thing is," she says, now sounding like Billy Chart, "that your Mob is Dionysian while we are Apollonian. The Mob believes in passion, cruelty, violence, destruction, indulgence, polarization, confrontation and pain as the means and methods of human affairs. We do not. We never have. Didn't you notice the change in things? We believe in reason, order, control, temperance, patience, the pastoral virtues. Discussion and engagement. The moderation and modification of the baser passions. If we tried to deal in the way that your Mob dealt we would lose all of our powers. We wouldn't be the Counters any more, we'd merely be another division of the Mob and that means that we couldn't possibly beat them. Then it would have to be the Mob that was ruling the world. We have to do it our way."

A female horseplayer comes over in slacks and a halter—I had not realized what a popular and loyal clientele Julie has acquired—and asks for a stick of Wrigley's chewing gum, very soft. "I'm sorry, she says, "this stand is closed."

"How can it be closed? It's never closed during the races."

"I'm off duty. I'm having a discussion."

"Yeah, you're making time, you bitch, making time with a cello player. Don't tell me; I know everything that's going on here, you people aren't happy rigging the races, you got to screw around too," the lady horseplayer says and goes away again or at least she disappears, leaving Julie shaking her head with a rather bemused expression. "That's exactly what I mean," she says, "this kind of generalized hostility and hatred. The crowds have never been more violent and pained. You can thank your Mob for that."

"Listen," I say, "stop calling it my Mob, it isn't nothing of the sort. A man in my occupation picks up certain obligations and responsibilities and has to deal with them through the means he has. The Mob was the only thing that there was, so I got involved. It wasn't nothing personal and I have nothing to do with the Mob one way or the other; it just worked out that way. Granted your argument that they're such evil."

"Oh, that's the pity of it," she says, sounding less and less like a Stevens lady or even a disturbed Stevens lady, "that's the pity of it: the evil, the malice, the way they work, they make couriers of you all and none of you ever feel culpable. It's diabolical. Diabolical! Surely, you should appreciate the opportunity you've been given. An outfit like this has to purely be put out of business."

"Leaving that to one side for the minute," I say, "there's another question.

Suppose I listen to you and I refuse to do it. I don't dig up the Flat which incidentally means that at midnight this evening or slightly before I am blown to sky-high ribbons or smithereens as they call it in Pop Warner's. So what? So what about it? All that they'll do is tomorrow to get someone else and the whole thing will happen again, don't you see? If it isn't me it will be some other guy so I don't understand what the point even is of taking this time with me. If I say no it will only be someone else."

"Ah," she says, "but that's the point too if you'll only think about it. That's precisely the point, don't you understand? You can only function for yourself. You can only make your decisions for yourself and go on from there. If you refuse to do it, then it means that the next one may refuse too. If enough refuse, it will eventually be too late and it doesn't matter whether he gets out or not. You live your life to yourself, no one else has the responsibility. You must do this one thing for yourself, that's all. Why worry about the others? That's Mob thinking. Think of the integrity of self."

"It's too much," I say and stand, reach for my cello case. "I'm a simple man. I went to Utica College a division of Syracuse University for a single semester back in 1957 but it never took and I decided that I'd probably be better off in the Army instead. I am not highly-educated. My opportunities are limited. I just don't know how much of this I can take." This is a perfect lie, of course. It is a true fact that, my educational disadvantages to the contrary, I have always considered myself a highly intelligent man who in different circumstances would have made lights go up in the intellectual world. Nevertheless, it seems time to terminate the discussion and if what Julie has said is to be interpreted truly, the Dionysian Apollonians or Apollonian Dionysians believe too much in temperance and moderation to stop me. "Thanks a lot," I say, "I'll think about it."

"I see I'll have to convince you," she says, "you won't listen to reason unsupported by myth and prophecy; it's an old habit but maybe in terms of your background it's a good one. Listen to the call of the second race. It will be won by number eight, Tinker Bell who will pay three dollars and forty cents to win, two sixty to place and two twenty to show. It should be on right now. Would that convince you?"

Standing, I feel somewhat better to say nothing of more control of the situation and I say, "I'll listen to anything."

"It's too late to bet if you're thinking of that kind of thing."

"Who bets even-money?" I say and at that moment, prophetically or otherwise, the amplifiers come on for the call of the second race and Caposella says that Tinker Bell in the middle of the track, takes the lead. The under-grandstand is almost empty, only a few senile old men and women wandering around with shopping bags looking for droppings and even fewer crazed optimists who pile onto the cashier's windows to collect their bets early in case they win. Julie yawns and leans back on her seat, feigning, as the word goes, an elaborate casualness and I follow Caposella's call with interest. As always it is characterized by its individuality and distinctiveness; Caposella's diction is the surest indication that nasality, contrary to medical superstition, does not lead to lower articulation or a reduced degree of intelligence. Tinker Bell, Caposella gives us to believe, leads by three lengths coming into the stretch turn and then begins to pull away. By herself, says Caposella, and I am willing on the merits of the case to believe this. The mumbles and grumbles refracted inside vanish and Caposella advises that the result of the race is not yet official and all pari-mutuel tickets must, please, be held and the amplifiers go off with a loud tick. I wish Caposella well and wonder whether he ever makes selections of his own or whether the public relations statements are correct and he is a dedicated non-bettor. Julie looks at me with a slow glow of triumph illuminating the corners of her face and taking some sort of the edge off the crinkles and says, "you'll find that the prices stand up. Does that convince you that we know what we're doing?"

I shrug, and hoist the case. I am about to try something difficult and totally out of context but on the other hand it has been a terrible set of times so far and every indication is that things will become even more difficult before the day is over. I am entitled to this. I am entitled to one gesture and as I start it I know instinctively that I will be able to carry this one thing off and that Harry the Flat himself would be truly proud of me.

"So," I say, looking at her and preparing for a magnificent striding exit, "so listen to me, what kind of organization have you got there that would go to three to five shots in a cheap race like this? What kind of minds operate there; don't you have any sense of humor? And besides that," I say, pointing at her with a distinct flourish, "besides all that, tell me how much real smarts it takes to call the winning and prices on a three to five shot? Answer me that, my smart lady, and by the time you do maybe I'll be able to give you the results of my decision on my poor, stinking friend the Flat who only deserves after all these times a decent burial and who was closely related to his widow by marriage for several years before his problems became insuperable."

And leave her standing that way, striding to the escalator, holding the case nimbly, like a violinist, even daring to wink at her when the steps begin to move. The escalator carries me skyward; vaulting above the crowd and Julie like this I feel for an instant as Tinker Bell herself must have felt only a minute or so before, throwing herself from her field for daylight, vaulting above them for her own brilliance, superseding the claimers behind her, as for once in my life, I have also superseded something, I suspect well, there will be no payoffs made on me.

It is all true, all too true, and by the time I have reached my seat again I have returned to a proper solemnity not to say trepidation as I begin to understand that the real thinking of the difficult afternoon now lies ahead of me to say nothing of the horseplaying too.

XXXIII

SAMPLE SYSTEMS OF HARRY THE FLAT

1) Play only maiden-specials, allowance races and lower grade handicaps. Claiming races and stakes must be discarded because there are less variables. Play the three horses in each race which go off at the longest odds on the board for five dollars to win and place. Double the amount bet after every loss but do not exceed three doublings, that is, bets of forty dollars, but after three losses return to the amount of original investment. If a hit is made in one of the first three races bet, take the money and immediately go home. Leave. Do not remain for any of the races. Do not even think of remaining for the following races. Do not parlay winnings. Only losings are to be parlayed.

2) Restrict play to bottom claiming races for fillies and mares, age three years and up. These should be races in which the claiming price of the most expensive horse in the race does not exceed five thousand dollars. Bet all horses in the race listed at odds of between eight to one and twenty to one to win and double the bet after every loss up to a maximum of forty dollars. A lower percentage of favorites win these than any other kind of races on the New York circuit, meaning that this system has a chance to win. Be reasonable however and if two or three eight to five shots come home in a row in these bottom filly races, then try to think of another system.

3) Play only cheap claiming races for mares, fillies, colts, geldings or ridgelings. Look for a horse which finished last in its previous race, next to last in the race before that and third from last in the race before that. This indicates that a trainer is maneuvering for a bottom performance from his horse in order to catch a big price. Bet such a horse to win and place and double the bet after every loss. This system gets enormous prices. Only three or four plays in a season will emerge but they will be on horses at prices ranging from seventy to one and up and should not be ignored.

4) Look for a horse which won its last race in a driving finish, that is by a margin of a length or less. Driving finishes tend to knock even better horses off form but the crowd doesn't know it; three times out of four, such a horse will be a favorite in its next race. Ignore that horse as long as its odds are less than three to one. Instead, dutch the book among the other logical contenders so that you will cash a bet no matter which one of them wins. Try this angle for repeaters.

5) Jockey system: play one of the ten leading jockeys on the circuit to win on every one of his mounts *after* he has lost ten races in a row. Top jockeys fall into losing streaks but these streaks rarely exceed six or seven in a row and when you find a leading jockey who has lost as many as ten you know that he is determined to win. Since the average losing streak for a jockey is 3.2 you

know that you have an excellent bet through this system. Double the bet after every loss and play straight progression here.

6) Play a horse that won its last race to win again if it is not moving up in class, won its last race by three lengths or more, is ridden by a top jockey, has a history of at least two back-to-back wins within the previous year, is not carrying more weight than it did in its previous victory, is running within five days of its previous victory and is listed on the board at odds of more than ten to one. Very few plays emerge through this system but those that do are worthwhile and should be awaited.

7) Hundred-dollar betting window system: shortly before post-time for the race, go to the one hundred dollar window and stand diffidently to one side, close enough to the window to hear the big bettors announce the numbers of the horses they are playing to the mutuels clerk. Most of the smart money comes in at the hundred dollar window and the most popular hundred dollar window is the grandstand; too many wise guys try this system in the clubhouse and tend to pick up only false information. The grandstand is the play therefore. It is important to remain nonchalant and at ease in front of the Pinkerton guard who stands by the hundred dollar window. He is there for precisely the purpose of protecting the hundred dollar bettors and if he feels that you are too obviously seeking information, he will ask you to move along. If he does this to you, comply without argument and discard the system for that week. Pinkerton guards change on rotation every week and therefore the system can be put into operation the following Monday. Be discreet. If you do pick up information, bet the horse you hear to straight win as big bettors are only interested in playing it on the nose. Parlay after losses. If three or more horses are heard played at the hundred dollar window skip the race; if only two, play them both to win. Try to be at the window as close to post-time as possible. It is wise to bring a cup of beer or coffee along with you to give the impression that you are merely having a bit of a snack and are not actually in pursuit of information.

8) Paddock system: stand by the paddock as the horses take the track before the race and listen to the paddock guard at the gate who often engages in friendly conversation with passers-by and some of the grooms who walk through the gate to make their own bets. Try to deduce, if he does not actually say, what his choice is for the forthcoming race and bet it. An alternative system is to try to cultivate the friendship of the Pinkerton guard by being in the same spot at the same time for several weeks, etc., until he takes you into his confidence. However rotations, illnesses and conflicting information from the grooms can make this system unsuccessful if played too singlemindedly.

9) Men's room system: attend the rest room between races, at that time when it is most crowded and ask the man at the next urinal who he is betting.

Leave the rest room and return five minutes later when there will have been almost total turnover and again ask the question. If the same answer is obtained twice, the horse is the bet. A correction-system calling for three straight selections of the same horse will cut down losses but reduce the prices.

10) Clocker Lawton system: Play Lawton's choice to win in every race on the nose. No progression, no doubling, no reduction. The same amount must be bet every time. If Lawton has a bad day, try the New York Turf Letter or Powell's Green Sheet.

XXXIV

SNAPSHOTS OF A MARRIAGE

Lying on my wife, working myself heavily into her, I feel myself edging into some kind of connection, some movement and blending that I have never known before and it is not the orgasm I feel overtaking me so much as a complex of emotions so moving that I know it will take me a long long time to sort it out. She moans against me, opens herself top and bottom, the panels of her skin slide roughly through me and I work myself through the last necessary inches, thinking of her, thinking of what we could have. But at the last moment, once again, the damned vision comes of jockeys and silks and colors and toteboards and flickering in the grandstand. Odds seem to sift in my ruined brain, to say nothing of program entries, and I feel myself moving away from her, moving further, weakening within her limbs and it is all shrinking, shrinking. Desperately, to avoid failure once again, I close my eyes and jounce upon her frantically, holding her limbs like reins, snorting in her ear and think of nothing but the need to finish, the necessity not to disgrace myself. Slowly, slowly, I feel myself rising, slowly the aged flowers below open up and almost without sensation, in a kind of catalepsy I pour my seeds into her, my eyes opening at the moment of immersion to stare at the blank, ruined surfaces of the wall. "I can't stand it anymore, I can't stand it," she says, but whether she is referring to what has just happened or all that went before, I did not know. I reapply myself the more gloomily to my tasks, finishing her as best I can in the only way I can finish her, hearing a flap like the pages of the *Telegraph* in the background signalling my separation from my more meaningful destiny.

Finding her in the act of dressing, her head cocked to an odd angle, confronting herself with a kind of astonishment in the mirror, I feel an emotion toward her I have not known for a long time, something midway between lust and protectiveness. I go over to her quickly, put my hand on her shoulder, feel the skin move up against me and then begin to circle downward, reach around, and cup her breast. It is then that the nipple retracts, seems to flare inward with a kind of eloquence she has never otherwise possessed, and she says, "get away from me, just get out of here; I'm dressing, can't you see that I don't want to be bothered?" "I want you," I say, which is strange because it is so rarely the case, but it is the case now. I can feel necessity lumpish in my trousers and say, "come here," and she says, "you've been at that whorehouse all day and now you want me? How can you say you want me?" and I say, "It isn't a whorehouse; it's a business, it's like everything else, it's a question of being systematic, that's all. It's a business. It's life. Surely it is, you've got to give me some credit." She wheels around, her breasts flopping on her chest, the slow dangling movement pressing me into further attention and she says, "How much did you lose today?" "I won," I say, "I won seventy-three dollars, a day's pay. I caught the seventh and I caught the eighth. Now come here," and reach toward her again and she gets up, backs from me, her palm against her mouth and says, "you bastard, do you really think that it makes any difference whether you won or lost? You can't seduce me with that crap, it's the whole system that I can't stand, what do you think I am? Something you pick up there, that's what you think." "There's no pickup, there's no sex," I try to say to her, but it is hopeless, it goes far beyond reason, there is no question of dialogue anymore because spreading over all her features as she backs into the wall is something with which I cannot contend, something which causes the heaviness within to flop uselessly with gravity, something which causes the very stomach to churn and I feel that I must leave the room. She is looking at me with the heightened, darkening terror I have seen in so many of the faces around the walking ring before the last race and I cannot take it anymore. I cannot take it. The seventy-three dollars is pointless if this is what it is doing to me. I feel that I must change my life but by the next morning everything is entirely different and several stops have opened up in the sixth through ninth races. It is only in the evenings when she can move me still and then only through a kind of memory.

I have read the note on the table twice and it says the same thing, it says that she is leaving because she no longer sees any hope for anything which can happen in the house. Numbed, I turn toward the refrigerator, perhaps a beer will help. . . but as I close the door, beer can in hand, I see her at the entrance to the kitchen holding her bags and she says, reaching toward me, "I couldn't do it, you bastard. I wanted to do it so much but I just couldn't, I can't leave you," and comes toward me. We press against one another, the damned can falling with a clatter, and I can feel her hands on me as they have not been in months, seizing, groping, scratching, that birdlike whisk of hands which will always be my most characteristic memory of her and right there in the kitchen, somehow, I do not know how, we manage to do it. It is good, it is better than it has been for a long, long time, and aching, gasping, we fall to the floor still clutching one another. "I can't leave you, I can't leave you," she cries, "you're impossible but you just need me so much," and I promise her then that things will be different, that they will not remain in this impasse forever, that I will, as a matter of fact, try to take an entirely different tack just as soon as possible, because only she is important, and that is the way we huddle for quite a time. The night is good too but in the morning I have to leave for the track and two days later she does leave me after all, no note this time just a scribble in lipstick on her vanity mirror THE HELL WITH THIS and maybe papers come and maybe they do not and maybe lawyers write and maybe they do not, but the track, like all central things, goes on and on and on, and only past the time of its necessity can I think of anything else. She was a gentle girl with luminous eyes; freckles all over her, even on her breasts and when she opened against me for the first time she made a sound like crickets and sighing took me into that deepest part of her, so filled with light and tumbling, that one could forget it was darkness.

XXXV

DEEP CONTEMPLATIONS BEFORE THE THIRD: WHAT WOULD THE FLAT HAVE DONE?

My seat in the grandstand is still unoccupied, despite the fact that in the haste of exiting I neglected to fold down a page of the *Telegraph* as a signal of my presence. This is not really unexpected; by the second race on weekdays, a certain kind of companionship has already established itself in this sparsely-settled section of the grandstand, and names, faces and identities tend to be established to say nothing of seating arrangements. Scattered around me seems to be roughly the same cast as previous although there are slight alterations. A pretty young girl and a rather nervous escort have taken the place of an old couple two rows behind and a strange woman slicing oranges and eating the peels is three seats down to my right, supplanting a musically-oriented gentleman who had whistled all the way through the first. All this is normal, however, there is turnover at the races just as there is in life and the basic circumstances remain the same. Only I have changed. I am, to tell the truth, distinctly unsettled.

The thing that I wish to do more passionately than anything else is to take some few moments off to myself and think the situation through, but this is not easy for several reasons. In the first place, the Needles bomb is now beginning to itch like crazy; I had had the best assurance of all the attending surgeons that I would not even notice it was there until and unless it blew up, but it is now a massive, heavy load sitting darkly in my thigh and sending out waves of tickling through the lower and upper limbs. It is the kind of tickling which might be entertaining if one were lying on a bed on a Sunday afternoon with nothing else truly to do but under these circumstances pretty unsettling. In truth the bomb is giving off sensations which I can only interpret as malfunction or imminent explosion and this does not lead to the kind of quiet reflection which has been recommended by Julie, the Dionysian Apollonian. In the second place, the third race, what with one thing and another thing, is almost upon me now and it is the third which was the object of some moderate interest last night; there is a horse in it named Social Scout who I have been following on and off for a year now and whose record is just bad enough and recently unsuccessful to make possible the question of maneuvering. I want to put ten dollars on Social Scout to win and thus have even more money to put on the ultimate tip of the eighth but there are other horses in the race too that I had noticed: No Monicker and Fast Cloud and Arabian Spy and Inch by Inch in particular. All of them have proven capable of winning in this company and all of them need that kind of careful investigation and separation in which I modestly specialize. All these distractions work against the lecture and instruction which I have received below just a few moments before.

Nevertheless, one must try to return order to one's existence even in the most difficult circumstances and therefore I work out a program. First, I extract the Mob's last ten dollars from the special Mob compartment of my wallet and while I finger it, look over the entries quickly. I decide that Social Scout might stand up in this company precisely because his record looks so awful, and hobble to the window to make my bet. It is then my intention to return to the seat, and in the four or five minutes before the third, give the whole question some very serious thought. But instead there are problems, my mind scuttles around in my head like a rat in a cage and instead of taking the breeze and working out factors in my seat I find myself doing some very serious thinking on the line to the ten dollar window, which is not the place to do serious thinking of any sort except selection . . . which selection is not truly serious thinking as any experienced horse player can tell you.

Jammed between a couple of thin types who have separated themselves and are exchanging confidences over my shoulder, I began to consider the question of the Counters versus the Mob. It is all very confusing because this business of the world being divided into two opposed types of people who battle over it, I have always felt to be associated with the youthful thinking of my retarded years and have instead tried to cultivate that mature weary sophistication which tells you that everybody is really part of two groups or perhaps three, depending upon whether or not he is also, in addition to all this, religious. Certainly nothing in my experience would make Julie's theory or truth stand up very well and yet there is a kind of horrifying realism to it. It is the kind of thing which just might work out if you looked at circumstances in a certain way. I am not the only person I know who feels that the world has gotten much worse since late 1963, but on the other hand this is more the personal than the political operating because it was in 1963 that I began to play the horses truly seriously. It is quite possible that 1963 was the year that a number of people decided to or were forced to stop playing them seriously, in which case the years since then would have seemed better rather than worse.

In short, everything is relative, a good perspective and one I have always tried to cultivate through thin circumstances and thick. I return to the figures on Social Scout, indulging in my usual window habit of trying to pick up some last bit of information or possibility which might spring the whole speculative nature of a bet into a good solid investment. But my concentration is broken by the question of Counters and Mob and also the two horseplayers spread out over me are having a furious argument of their own over the merits of the race to come, an argument of which I become slowly more and more aware, like sniffing gas odors during sleep or becoming cognizant of the fact that one is missing a limb. "Arabian Spy," the one in front says, "the figures on Arabian Spy confirm. He had a thirty-two windage."

"That's absolutely true," the one behind me says, gesturing in such a fashion that he taps my shoulder blade painfully, "but the windage factor is not an absolute in terms like this, considering the level of weight carried and the outage of the track, the banking interval alone ought to cut down the windage fifty-five percent. You can't credit him with more than a twenty-three windage and that's at the outside. Fast Cloud has to get the plus marks on bankage so where are you?"

"Where are you, where are you, who the hell knows?" the one in front says, jamming his finger at the *Telegraph* and slamming me uneasily in the ribs as the line moves forward a notch, "there ain't no easy answers but the horse broke in the last time and the bolting consideration has got to be invoked. There is an eighty-two percent possibility of going wide on the turn by any figures you use."

"But the horse goes to the outside to accelerate, you can check the leverage," the one behind says and knees me rather violently in the rear of a joint, causing me to stumble, virtually toppling over the cello case. It is really too much, all too much for me, "for God's sake, gentlemen," I find myself saying, as I pull the case to rigidity and advance another couple of paces, "you've got to cut this out; there's a man in the middle here. You want to get together, drop behind me but show a little courtesy."

"He wants us to show some courtesy," one says and the other says, "this man believes in courtesy," and they turn on me then with curiously blunt faces, blunt and intense, the eyes piercing behind the flesh. For all the world they look to me like a thousand men I have seen in the back rooms of Tony Winner and I can feel myself virtually bracing, shuddering in some sudden breeze which seems to come in through the flapping doors. "Make your bet," I say, indicating that the line has indeed broken for us and the man in front is now at the window. "Make your bet and forget the whole thing, will you?"

"A cellist," the man says, "this guy's a fucking cellist and he's telling us how to play the horses." He leans over to the clerk, whispers something, regards me with distinct loathing as he takes a ticket and stuffs it into his pocket. "You better keep your mouth to yourself, cellist," he says.

I go to the window, put down the ten on Social Scout and turn away, prepared to go back to my seat but find that my way is blocked by the two of them who have intercepted my way and hands on hips are looking at me with decided grimness. "We don't need lectures on manners, cellist," one says but maybe it is the other: like so many of the people who come in to discuss matters with the Winner they are relatively interchangeable and it is hard to see whether I am dealing with the one who pushed me or who I warned. In any event, I have a rising disinterest in finding out. Something turns off dully in me and virtually all the way and I can feel a kind of sinking cowardice I have not known for a long, long time. It is not so much that I have gone through recent years without fear as that the more distinctly physical elements of it have been rubbed off by subtler horrors. "Cut it out," I say, "cut it out," but they do not seem disposed to cut it out at all. This is impossible: who among other people, would run into danger of physical assault in the grandstand at Aqueduct and on this of all the crucial days? One of them reaches out a fondling, investigative hand toward my thigh and touches randomly and urgently in the area roughly above the locale of the time bomb and it is at this moment that something within me breaks, I blow more than a smithereen or two of my unnatural composure and backing away I shriek at them in what seems to be a dismaying falsetto although I try not to pay too much attention; "cut it out, will you? Lay off me, huh? If you want a tip I'll give you a tip, just leave me the hell alone and I'll give you something worthwhile."

"He wants to give us a tip, Bertram," one of them says and they look at one another with grins, then wheel back to stare at me. "A tip. You really look like a tipster cellist."

"But I am, I am," I say, wondering how many years ago this scene occurred; surely it must have been twenty or so, it could not be happening now, "Listen to me and it'll be worth your while. Knockover in the eighth. Bet Knockover. He's going to be a hundred to one, two hundred to one off the board and believe me, he's worth it."

"Knockover," one of them says. He turns to his companion and smiles, smiles ever so gently and then the other begins to laugh, setting off the first and then they are laughing very hysterically indeed but perfectly within control, if you know what I am saying. "Knockover, he's giving us Knockover, my God, where'd you pick that one up, cellist? It's all over the lot; you must have heard it in the men's room or maybe I am thinking of that crazy bartender down on the first level or maybe it would be clubhouse Annie. Knockover, Knockover, the *cellist* is giving us Knockover now, is it a sign?" and they laugh and laugh, it is desperate and humiliating but leaves one particular note of optimism which I am quick to take advantage of, their laughter distracts them. Or maybe it is only that they too are willing to get out of this gracefully, and in either event, I scuttle away rapidly, head down, moving rapidly toward the open air. They let me go and I stagger back to my seat hoping that they will take no heed of angles or numbers and it is only as I get to the seat again that I understand what they have told me and what the consequences of this might be.

But there is no time to think of that. This is not my day, it would seem or at any rate, it is a day founded completely upon distraction. Waiting for me at my seat is David, my companion from last evening, and he has a very determined look upon his face, a look of determination that seems to turn to purpose as I approach and before I can even take possession of my seat again his arms are upon me, although somewhat more gently. "There you are," he says, "I been waiting for you. Where were you? gone to make a bet."

"Yeah," I say, "I thought I'd watch the race," referring to the fact that the starting gate is now half-full of horses who are about to break. "If I could."

"Well you can't," he says, "I'm sorry but you got to come with me right now. The boss wants to talk to you this minute; he got reports and he wants to see you and I'm supposed to take you, so make things easy and come along."

"But I can't!" I say, "the Winner is in the clubhouse and I never been in the clubhouse in my whole life!" Perhaps this is not the most rational way to put it, but my reasons are explicit if not my language. "Listen, everything's all right."

David reaches within his pockets, extracts a soiled grey tie and hands it to me. "That takes care of the clubhouse part," he says, "and for the rest of it, I got my orders and you better come right along now or you will be extremely regretful. I hate to be this way but you got to understand that's the way the operation goes, I got to follow my instructions and that's all there is to it. Come on, come on, I'll take the cello case," and as nimbly as Toscanini ever could, he snatches it from my hands, grabs me by a wrist and leads me through the rows of the grandstand, toward the exit and easterly, toward the domain of Tony Winner.

I follow. It is purely a question of geophysics.

XXXVI

GERTRUDE NEE HAWKINS SUBMITTING
TO HARRY THE FLAT: THE QUESTION
OF CONFLICTING LIFESTYLES

Underneath him, feeling the poised frenzy of his body, his skin slipping smoothly away from her as fast as she can grasp it, she feels that she may have reached some kind of accommodation, that it may, after all, have worked out all right. Harry has her, now and then, to enact his passions upon, such as they are, and as far as she goes, she has the ceiling. The ceiling is dense and white, scarred and faintly pitted, it looks like Harry's flesh although far more distant and resilient and she feels that if she can concentrate upon it profoundly enough, everything more immediate will go away. In addition she will have absorbed from this precarious balance the kind of lesson which will alter the entire context of her life: she will become a different person. "Oh God," the Flat murmurs, running a finger through her hair, twisted off into some intricate alley of his own pursuit, and absently she pushes back. Gertrude dangles a reciprocal hand at the back of his scalp, feels the faint warmth emanating from the back of his neck, feels the timing of his grunts as they come from the deepest, most bound part of him. How hard he is working upon her, and for such fragile outcome! But Gertrude does what she can, listens to the surge of his blood, coaxes him past rising, thinking that if she can only get past the next few moments then it is all downhill from here on. But looking at the ceiling again she finds that it is receding, tracking in some kind of elliptical orbit around her and then she understands that she has been flung upon her belly again. The bastard will not leave her alone when he gets in a certain mood, must have things in his own fashion. She closes her eyes, feels the graze of blankets, the whisk of sheets as they slide past her cheeks and tries now to cleanse herself of all thought. However the tickling pressure begins between her legs and his high, whining moans: this is the worst part of it. It happens only now and again but when it does it is enough to back her off any sense of it. She finds herself wondering with some detached portion of the mind exactly what she is doing here and what she could have had in mind when she decided to marry him. Was this all she wanted? But his tongue, if no other part of him, knows its purposes, cleaves in and out. Sighing, she squeezes her thighs, shakes her head, takes a deep breath . . . and feels him mount her, sobbing. Now, at last, it is almost over, it is only a question of getting through the next minute or so and then it will all be over. She feels his hands moving underneath her breasts, tearing, rising, gripping and bites her lip not in pain but for the sheer embarrassment of it. What could anyone think of her if they saw her now? He begins to move upon her unrhythmically, broken motion, talking to himself; she clamps her thighs to trap him and feels him slide halfway up. Enough, enough. Now he is talking once again; it happens every so often and that too is predictable and must be gotten through. He is talking about colts and geldings, fillies and mares in a husky, trapped voice, murmuring something about odds and angles and track circumference, and at the moment when his lecture reaches its quickest and most insistent point—but not before, oh no, never before, there is just no way around this—he spills into her grunting, dry, hard, bitter trickles. She sobs in sheer gratitude for this completion and he rolls off her, his eyes closed, breathing unevenly, looking up at the ceiling—*her* ceiling—and for the sheer anguish of it she curls against him and puts her head on his chest and he holds her neck in a gentle thumb clasp. That is the only way the two of them go to sleep. Another day at the races over for Harry the Flat, and a rare one too—for rarely can he afford such special connection.

He is not much, but at least he is there, and for whatever reason, he is all that she now has. She tries to comfort herself with this but it is not easy and when her thoughts, as they have been doing more and more, lately, move toward sleep in a welter of horses, whinnies, calculations and slide-o-meters she knows that something definite will have to happen soon, because she, too, is approaching her limits. But time enough for that tomorrow, sleep at last and seven hours or a little more until she has got to get out of bed and she will take it, she has to take it, she guesses that she will take it as long as necessary.

This is my interpretation of certain scenes in the marriage between Gertrude nee Hawkins and Harry the Flat. It is not necessarily the absolute truth but it is sufficient for me and it is as far as I care to take it now, or for that matter, ever.

XXXVII

A DISCUSSION IN THE CLUBHOUSE: THE ISSUE IS PUT CLEAR, THE FOURTH PROVIDES ANOTHER SURPRISE

Up until what might as well be called the imminent moment, it is a fact that I have never been in the clubhouse, at Aqueduct or anywhere else, in my entire life. The only difference between the clubhouse and the grandstand, as far as I can see reputed, is that the clubhouse costs five dollars to enter and the grandstand two. This difference, of its own, imposes some kind of automatic segregation, not to be otherwise understood, except in terms of the neckties men are supposed to wear. Horseplayers who think nothing of betting an extra three or thirty dollars at the last moment apparently think greatly of an additional expenditure at the outset. Therefore, what you get in the clubhouse, or in any event, what I think you get is a different class of people, more sparse than those in the grandstand and, in my opinion, of a different order altogether. I tend to think of them as not being serious types in relation to horseracing and lacking the kind of application which you will find throughout the grandstand. On the other hand, as far as I know, there are fewer crazy ladies in the clubhouse and the men on fine days are less apt to denude themselves to the legal limit to take advantage of the beneficial rays of the inner tote board, striking fire into their flesh.

All of this may be prejudice, there is no way for me to be sure of anything as psychologically explosive and profound as the reasons why I have feared throughout my life to enter a clubhouse. Once, while performing a minor service for Tony Winner at Saratoga some years ago, I almost found it necessary to go into the clubhouse to get a large bet down at an uncrowded window, but the sight of three or four young girls in necklaces, sleeveless dresses and a fine, cold look around the eyes, as they stared at my imminent entrance, was enough to send me straight around and back to the grandstand where I was able, in the final analysis, to get the bet down after all. (The horse ran out, which made the Winner distinctly uncomfortable, but I had the tickets and the papers had the proof and there was really nothing that he could do to me.) Since then I have never been even in that vicinity again.

I am aware, as would be any horseplayer of my means, experiences and backgrounds, that there is not a single class of horseplayer but in fact two, and that this other class, which has nothing to do with me, is as important and central and necessary to the game as my part. I also realize that this other class believes itself to be at least as serious as I, but somehow I am unable to pay them the true and fine cognizance of wanting to mingle with them. This sec-

ond class, which is composed of people who come to the races to spend
money rather than to win it, is responsible for most of the horses and most of
the races and most of the spectator aspects of racing but, as I say, I try to have
as little to do with it as possible. I stay in more meaningful niche, and if I never
went to a clubhouse in a hundred years, I believe I would be duly satisfied.
Particularly, it had never been my expectation that I would find myself vis-
iting a clubhouse in precisely this way: supporting a cello case, limping with
a bomb sewn in my thigh, led by a short, tough man with square shoulders
and a determined stride whose eyes were never deserted by a certain merry
light which could well be madness. Two or three times, on the long walk
through the infield, the thought has occurred to me to take evasive action. It
would not be difficult to slip his gaze, dodge a handhold and amalgamate myself into the hordes of horseplayers who are studying their possibilities at all
angles before the windows, but a certain aspect of David's gaze assures me that
this would not be wise. Then too, evasive action would not be very bright since
good relations with the Winner remain as essential as always. Only through
the Winner's graces, after all, will the faithful George Needles find himself
induced to remove the timing device.

On the other hand again, one must have three hands to be any kind of a decent horseplayer, but if the question of the Counters is one to be taken seriously, then perhaps the Winner's graces or Needles' faith are not to be taken
into account as confidently as previous. In any event, one way or the other,
I stay with David the Assistant who winds me here and winds me there and
eventually takes me to the junction between grandstand and clubhouse
where, under the gaze of some exceeding grim guards, one is permitted to pay
three dollars for the transfer and move over directly to the Holy Land. The
fact that these guards exist always as a periphery, seeing the two different
classes of horseplayers rushing by them on either side and unable to make any
judgment as to their own status (although they stand on the clubhouse side
to be assured), makes them particularly surly and there is one very bad moment when I try to push my way through in David's wake. He has shown his
invisible-ink handstamp to the guard and gone through. I take it for granted
that my way has been planned as well, but the guard stops me with a terrific
thrust to the cello and says, "Where do you think you're going, friend? Giving a guitar concert?"

"It's a cello," I say, insisting upon this nicety once again. I cannot stand to
hear musical instruments miscalled and people who call orchestras "bands"
or vice-versa irritate me more than practically any other kind because there
is no excuse for lacking this kind of precision.

"I don't care what it is, where the hell do you think you're going?"

"You have to pay," David says, looking at me from the other side. "He
means that you have to pay the three dollar differential."

"I thought that it was taken care of," I say and then understand that in a certain sense it is indeed taken care of and in any event Poughkeepsie, New York is also filled with barflies and welfare recipients who trusted to Tony Winner's instincts and humane nature. I extract three dollars of the Mob's money from my wallet and put it in the guard's hand, take another look of absolute hatred from him and step through. "Listen," the guard says, "there ain't supposed to be none of that stuff playing in the clubhouse. You ain't going to give concerts and beg pennies, are you?"

"No," I say, "I don't really play the cello, it's just something I am converting over to my sister's use after the ninth race."

"People could get very disturbed hearing string music during races. People could get very upset because this is not what they came to the races to hear and they might find it something of a distraction. I would advise you—"

"I think he understands, pal," David says and this for some reason quiets the guard instantly and completely. I drag the case through and we proceed toward a self-service clubhouse elevator. "I always been afraid of these things," David says, pointing to the invisible-ink on the back of his right hand, which of course I cannot see, "I always was afraid that they could give you skin cancer or maybe even bone cancer: how the hell do we know? How do we know what's really going on with this stuff? They got to use x-rays to look at it too, I think the whole thing is very dangerous. There are a whole lot of things they're starting to mess around with that we don't understand at all, not that anybody listens to my theories." We enter the elevator which is manned by a tiny operator wedged against a corner to such seeming invisibility that it could almost be self-service. "All the way up," he says, "the Winner's box," and the dwarf emits a high peep, closes the doors and slowly, groaning, we begin our ascent. The car shakes, David's teeth seem to chatter a bit in the machinery. "You never been up this way before, have you?" he says, "It's a new thing."

"That's right."

"The Winner is high, real high, he's even above Caposella's booth. You ever met Caposella?"

"No," I say, "I never had any curiosity."

"A lot of guys seem to say that," David says, "it's kind of interesting how many decide that Caposella is a voice and just leave it like that. Actually he's a very nice guy, although he don't understand nothing, but absolutely nothing, about the science of horse-racing." The dwarf peeps again and the doors slowly separate themselves, I find that we are looking into an alley so dense and grey that it seems to have absolutely nothing to do with the track and David urges me forward gently, speeding me out of the car. "The Winner is real high up," he says, "take my word of advice and don't look down," which I do, of course, immediately and regret it at once because the Winner appears to be not only on the roof of the clubhouse but several stories above it. We are apparently in a large tower enclosed by glass which looks down upon the clubhouse from a long distance. Beneath that is the paddock and then the track itself and it is miniaturized, at a great remove. It is a Track Under Glass, so to speak, with all the fixings, and I feel vertigo and nausea overtaking me by turns, and desperately clutch onto the neck of the cello which is also swaying. "He's high up," David says cheerfully and takes me through a door and into a small open-air section. In the middle of this box sits the Winner, surrounded by sheets of paper containing calculations and computations. He is dangling field glasses from his neck and wearing a very sharp blue blazer indeed which brings out all his famous and latent viciousness. "Here he is, Boss," David says, "it wasn't too much trouble at all getting him," and before the Winner has even sufficiently raised his head, deserts the box with a clatter, pulling some glass into place behind him. I shake my head and try to keep it down, fixating on the low bench on which the Winner sits mumbling and jotting figures on cards. He does not seem discomfited at all and only this gives me some hope as he finally looks at me saying, "Oh yeah, I see. Sit down, will you? You might as well." I sit on the bench next to him, it creaks and reels slightly under the impact and there is a single terrifying instant when I feel that I might have unbalanced everything by my presence and all of it: cello case, box, bench, supports. The Winner and I might go to the paddock in the quickest way but the Winner's ease is so bland, his absorption so complete that of itself it is almost something to hang on to. Finally, he turns and looks at me up and down and taking the sheets, begins to stack them two-handed. "All right," he says, "we got to do a little talking, that's the reason I brought you here. It won't take too long. Do you like my environs?"

I say without thinking that I like his environs very much. Indeed, it is easy to see under the circumstances of unusual strain or not, that the Winner takes great pride in his surroundings which, whatever their advantages or disadvantages, have the overwhelming power of exclusivity. It is the clubhouse with a vengeance, no question about it and in these circumstances even the Winner seems to have changed physically: he looks taller, broader, more concrete in the organic sense and seems to fit into the furniture of the box in a way that he never quite fitted into the back room of Pop Warner's, having a certain ease and contentment to the crossing of the legs. This is always the sign, in women too, of feeling that they have found themselves a spot from which they can play from strength. The Winner's confidence however seems to be a little thin around the edges, his eyes are a trifle duller than I remember them being and also his voice is hoarse, much unlike the smooth persuasive voice of the Winner who has taken me down so many alleys and byways in my time. "Listen here," he says, "the word around is that you're getting cold feet. Now you'd better not blow this one, character, or you'll be in trouble."

"How'd that get around?" I say, trying to maintain a certain calm, I know how important this is and even the physical surroundings must not counteract it. "I'm just doing my job."

"Time to level, time to level," grunts the Winner and reaches a hand in one of his pockets, crumples paper within and then removes it, shaking the hand from the wrist so that it appears curiously limp and detached. "Time to level, you been sitting down having a long confidential talk with that Juliet bitch who works out of Stevens and she's filled you full of a lot of lies and crap. You better not listen to that lady, she's crazy as hell and Stevens would pension her off if it weren't for the union. But they figure that she adds some color."

"I don't know nothing," I say, "I just came here on time and been playing the races. I spoke to her but I couldn't very well not speak to her, could I? Consider my position. I don't even remember too good what she was saying."

"It's all crap," the Winner says and raises a hand to his forehead to shield his eyes from the sun as he looks down at the twinkling paddock, the stick figures of horses now feeding into it, "it's all a lot of crap, there's no two organizations, there ain't nothing like that at all. Even the Mob is overrated. We don't control nothing, we're just trying to make a few bucks from predictions and with the help of the Chart, that's all. She can't fill you full of that garbage because it don't mean nothing. She mention the business about the Counters?"

"Something like that," I say. Tony Winner is definitely discomfited: I would put his twitchings and palpitations upon the seat down to indigestion or diarrhea, if I did not know his constitution so well, to say nothing of his habit of eating very little until the end of a working day, and then with great caution, under Needles's direction. "I don't remember any of it too good."

"Well," the Winner says, in the midst of the twitches, "it's all a lot of crap, that's what it is; you shouldn't even think none about that. There ain't no two organizations and there ain't no struggle between them and we don't run nothing. I know that's what she said to you because she's a crazy lady and that's the kind of stuff she spreads around to everyone who'll listen. She used to work in the clubhouse a long time ago but finally the patrons got fed up with the craziness so they put her in the grandstand where it wouldn't make no difference, that's all."

"She said," I say, "she said that I wasn't going to be saved in any event. She said, I mean, that whether or not I did the job, the time bomb was going to stay in the leg, in either case, because that was the way that you operated."

"Nonsense," the Winner says with a jerk, convulsing his shoulders, "that's nonsense; of course we'll take it out. It's only a little commission, a little job. An assurance, say. We always have to do it, it's a matter of policy, but just as soon as it's accomplished you'll come right back and Needles will have it out in two minutes and thirty seconds. Look at that bastard three," the Winner shrieks, breaking off the train of his monologue and leaping to his feet, "look at that son of a bitch, he's acting up in the paddock. Goddamn it to hell, he's so twitchy he'll never make it!" The booth sways frighteningly and I cling on for a handhold; the Winner, however, leans precariously and uses his field glasses to stare down at the paddock. "Can't stand it," he says, "I can't stand it anymore. How can he be acting up like that? It's all out of control."

"Was it the thing that he is supposed to win the race?" I ask which is possibly a dangerous question, "is he the one you want to win?"

The Winner's face clots and he sits abruptly, causing the booth to shake a little more, looks at me with a distinctly dangerous expression. "Shut up," he says, "just shut up and stop speculating; it is time that you came to terms with the fact that you are nothing but a messenger assigned to do one kind of job and that you had better do that job and keep your nose to yourself. You'd better get some consideration and some sense of proportion, you, look at that son of a bitch down there. He's gonna kick the groom to shreds. Halter him, will you!" the Winner screams and lunges precipitately toward the rail, almost losing his balance in the act of concentration. It is only simple justice or maybe I mean simple humanity that makes me rise to my feet against my own terror and drag him back to safety or at least to the bench upon which the two of us sit. Shaking his head he drops the glasses to his lap and looks at me with a kind of disgust; spaces in the disgust, however, show a different emotion which I have not really come to associate with the Winner. "The hell with it," he says, breathing hard, "it's just a little spot play, just a spot play, that's all. Listen you, you getting cold feet or anything?"

"I don't understand," I say, "I just don't get it; they took me down under pressure and made me have this little talk with that woman but why the concern you have—"

"It is all nonsense," the Winner says, "all complete nonsense, there is no such organization as the Counters. Why, those people couldn't get themselves arrested, let alone run things. How you could take that seriously is beyond me. Hey you, listen to me, when that eighth race comes along you'd just better do your job and forget about thinking—"

"I don't get it," I say, "in the first place I was only listening, not talking and in the second, why do I have to do it? I mean, what's the difference; there must be a hundred guys the Mob could have hired to do a job like this and I don't understand why it's so important to you that I do it." This kind of discussion with the Winner is perhaps dangerous; I am well aware of the fact that Syracuse, New York to say nothing of Oswego County are populated with a large number of obscure tramps and brain-damaged oldsters who have at one time ventured to discuss metaphysics with the Winner. Still, there is something in his voice and manner to indicate that he is possibly not as much in control of the situation as it would seem, and there is another factor which, as they say, extrudes. That factor is, that I am getting damned sick and tired of the Winner: sick and tired of the Mob and the Counters and threats and timebombs and George Needles and even Harry the Flat (may his soul still rest in peace, my feelings for him beyond this temporary irritation continue to run very strong). Although this would hardly be the time or place to let those feelings come to the fore, it is also a vivid truth that unless I do it now I am likely not to do it. There seems to be very little future in protest, on the other hand there is very little without it. "I mean, I know I'm in trouble," I say, "and that really you're doing me a favor in letting me bail out and all that, but I just don't understand why you got to put the screws on like this. Don't you trust me? Don't you think that I'll go through with it? Or do you think that somebody else might try to stop me?"

"That is enough," the Winner says, peering over the rail once again toward the paddock where the horses are beginning to string out toward the track, "that is distinctly enough of that line of reasoning."

"Because you're all wrong if you think that they'd try to stop me that way; this woman made it very clear that they don't function in that fashion. She said that she could only put forth the argument and leave it up to me to make the decision as to whether or not I would cooperate with them. She said that they used absolutely no force, that this was not their method at all being Apollonian Dionysians, or of that order."

"Apollonian," the Winner says. "Call it right. Apollonian."

"What's that?"

"Forget it. Oh, Jesus Christ, he's starting to run off now," the Winner says, totally abandoning the thread of our discussion as the number three horse breaks from the pack and begins to sprint toward the stretch turn with some speed and dedication. The jockey, a tiny stick figure crouched over it, is trying desperately to hold the reins in place as the horse goes out a further notch. Outriders catch up to the animal and begin to ease it back into place, the rest of the field circles it at some great distance. The Winner runs a hand through his lush hair and looks at me with such open despair in his eyes, such a remarkable expression for this familiar face, that I find it almost impossible not to say, "having some trouble with your selection, is that right Tony? You just can't control him too good anymore can you?" but in fact I do not say this, retaining not only some fragments of elemental caution, but also a real fear of the Winner's left hook. "They'll get him under control," I assure him instead, "these outriders here are certainly literally the best in the country and if the horse has any chance to win they will reserve his resources."

"Yeah," the Winner says, "yeah sure, that is very comforting to know but the fact is that I am all of a sudden and completely becoming bored with your presence here in my box and I do not want to continue this discussion anymore. Oh Jesus, now he's starting to rear. Don't throw the jockey, Jesus, please. I have finished imparting to you that information which now is necessary and I think that you should leave as quickly as possible and return to your place in the grandstand to prepare yourself against action."

"But why?" I say, "why that? I mean, wouldn't it be safer and better for you to keep me right here, under your eye, until the eighth if you don't trust me? I just don't follow." This too is dangerous material but I am in an inquisitive mood and the adventures of the number three horse have done Tony's assurance and stolidity no real good. In fact, although this is not a phrase I would use loosely, he seems to be something of a broken man, or at least considerably reduced from what I would like to think of as the Winner's Vigor. "I thought I'd just ask that anyway, I mean you don't have to tell me."

"I will not answer that because it is self-evident. This box is half a mile above the ground and at least a full mile from the area where you will conduct your activities . . . there would not be sufficient time for efficiency. Then too—" and Tony seems about on the point of imparting some even more important information, perhaps a moral code or a summation of my responsibilities and obligations. But as to the nature of this and my true relationship to him and what appeal he might make to me from the heart, I will never know because the three horse rears all the way into the air, skitters sidewise, tosses his jockey and then rolls heavily on the ground itself, having totally lost balance, just missing the jockey in the act of scrambling away. Kicking and struggling on the ground, the horse looks like a windup toy that has come loose, and as the outriders abandon the rest of the field to have a look, it strikes me and probably the Winner that the horse has had an injury. It cannot get up. "Oh my God," the Winner says, "my God, nothing's right. Nothing works. Nothing works anymore at all. There goes the whole spot."

"I think that horse has broken its back," I say.

"I don't give a shit if it's broken its head, will you look at that, I never seen nothing like that in my whole life. I'll kill the Chart. I'll kill him for this. He can't do it to me. Where is that son of a bitch?" And the Winner stands, flexes his wrists, runs a hand over the back of his head and then moves toward the exit door. "I have things to do," he says, "which demand my full attention for a little while but remember I will be back here long before the eighth and I will expect to see justice done. I will expect to see you function. I am leaving you now but I would not, in short, try any funny business. I'll kill that Chart right where he lays, the son of a bitch," the Winner says and makes an exit somewhat more graceless than his best, but even the bad ones, as happens to be the case with most of the influential people I know, are pretty effective.

I sit uneasily in the Winner's box for a few moments—the view is dizzying but I doubt very much that I will be back and it is an extremely favorable location—to watch the events taking place on the track, which from this viewpoint seem as consequential as an artifact or a child's game. A hacker's truck comes, shielding the horse from view and two men with rifles come out of it. From this vantage point there is no pain in it, it seems only puzzling that men should shoot horses. There is no sound whatsoever and if there are any crowd noises or discussions surrounding the shot they cannot be heard. Something in a sheet is passed into the trunk by ten struggling man and the truck drives off. Now, from this enormous height, all seems quiet, pastoral, removed, only the colors of the horses on the opposite side of the track, moving into the gate, breaking the gentle greens and greys and blues of the nature scene below. At this height one feels both removed from and impelled toward the action; suspended from it at such a remove that it is totally in control, involved enough with it to see it for the series of tiny and pointless manipulations that I always felt God would take horse-racing to be. To the extent that I ever got God involved with the question of horse-racing at all.

It is a very privileged site, a very privileged location that the Winner has in his box and I wonder if this is something that comes with the other privileges or whether it is the box that makes things possible. The whole thing is too deep for me and I find suddenly I do not want to consider any of it, I do not want to think anymore, I only want to get out of this box and back to the grandstand with which, at least, I can deal: can embrace a set of factors and understand them. I am not a person for the clubhouse, particularly not for this section of the clubhouse.

So I do something then which I have never done in my whole life. Just as the horses are about to break from the gate for the fourth, the whole race spread out in front of me, I spring to my feet, turn my back upon the upcoming horse-race, put the horse-race out of my mind completely with the turning and I leave. I do not care what happens. I want only to get back to my place in the grandstand and try to make decisions.

I do not care what is happening down there. If this was a response I had inaugurated about ten years ago, I would have led an entirely different life, but then too I would not have been able to appreciate what a truly remarkable step this has been.

David is not there to escort me, and the elevator, minus the Winner's presence, has lost its dwarf. It is completely self-service but it is waiting for me and drops me half a mile from the sky at terrific speed, into the waiting jaws of the clubhouse Exacta window line where I cannot leave soon enough. The guard offers me a free invisible-ink tattoo so that I can return to the clubhouse any further time that day, at will, but I tell him although I appreciate this, I think I will pass it up. Gesturing emphatically I almost drop the cello case once again on his toe but recover in time. Before the possibility of further dialogue, I make a hell of a hasty exit, indeed, into the pocket of my beloved grandstand.

XXXVIII

CATHOLICISM AS A COMFORT TO
GERTRUDE NEE HAWKINS

Although the Flat was a lapsed Catholic and made no bones about it, Gertrude found particularly in the last years of her marriage, that her religion was an enormous comfort to her and sustained her through periods that otherwise she would not have been able to bear. "Oh Jesus, Mary and Joseph," she would say in front of the crucifix-and-offertory which she had had installed, at some expense, in her own bedroom, "Jesus, Mary and Joseph, I simply can't take any more of this, I pray to all the saints to show me the way; I can't stand it. There must be something other than this to life. The man is completely insane and I'm too young to end up this way," she says and the crucifix wafts slowly in the breeze of her breath, giving her the distinct feeling that her appeal was being heard. Even if very little could be done to rectify her situation it was good to know that at least someone was listening to it and proving sympathetic. "Oh God, it's sinful, it's iniquitous, there must be another way," she would say on long summer afternoons when they were running at Saratoga and the Flat was forced to commute all-the-hell-the-way to Atlantic City, "please do something to him so that he will understand what has become of us and make him change. Or strike vengeance into his heart, either way, either way." Although Gertrude had, like most Catholics, had some formal instruction in ritual and formal Latin when she was a child, most of this had gone by the boards after her confirmation and now she was forced to rely upon simple Latin phrases, the one or two she knew, and basic appeals and complaints given in her own language. "Kyrie Eleison, there's got to be a way out of this," she would say or "Dominus Vobiscum, break down every single one of his parlays," or "Pater Noster, may every horse he bets on run last." Sometimes her prayers were answered but then again sometimes they were not; the Flat was relatively close-mouthed about the details of his routine performances. In any event, Gertrude knew that she would be in there now until the finish, she was praying seriously and thinking in the long term.

The Flat of course would tend to mock her religiosity and would, on those rare occasions when she was stupid in her timing and he happened to interrupt her in prayer, become out-rightly insulting. Once he tore the crucifix from the wall and flung it at her, narrowly missing the bridge of her nose, saying, "for God's sake, will you put your faith in something meaningful and try to give me some help instead of this nonsense!" Then he would proceed to curse her so variously and awfully that Gertrude understood that he was offended as only a deeply religious man could be, and actually envied her her ability to get down on her knees and pray for assistance. "I tell you, I won't have any more of this, ever," he would say on those occasions when he would have sex with her. It was always, at her insistence, in her bedroom and under the very glint of the crucifix whose aspect the Flat could not avoid, close his eyes and hunch his shoulders as he might. "It just gives you the willies," he pointed out to her, pleading for her to at least cover it with a cloth or go into his bedroom but she was determined. If the Flat would not respond to her prayers in any other fashion, he would at least see their results. Of course it is possible that she did not phrase this quite so eloquently.

Sometimes, he would come home having hit a small double or successfully chased a ten dollar win parlay through a couple of races. Then he would grin at her, flick coins and bills in the air, and narrow his face to that penetrating squint which the Flat always took on when he felt he had the game at least temporarily licked. When he did this she would absolutely despair, would feel in some dim recess that she was making a fool of herself and that her problems, to say nothing of Harry's were out of reach of the simple saints she could reach. But then there would be nights when he would stagger in past midnight, his face cold and empty, eyes winking death and would go straight to his bedroom muttering and she would know that something was being done; that in whatever fashion, her interests were being considered in that vault where, one way or the other, everyone, sooner or later, came under the glass.

That was all right with her. She was not frivolous. She was not indulging herself or using religion as a cheap release, as Harry had unfairly accused her of doing. Her purposes were serious. Her dedication was steadfast. She was, as a matter of fact, in this thing all the way and was not quitting until she saw some real results.

It was like investing. You put something in and stayed with it and sooner or later you hoped that it would come back, everything you had put in and a little interest too. If she could parlay trouble for the Flat, with a little interest for herself as well, that was all the better, but she didn't want to get greedy about the matter; she would take things in her stride. Take them as they came. Play with the booking percentages.

XXXIX

BACK TO QUARTERS FOR THE FINAL
TIME: THE GRANDSTAND LIKE
THE VAULT OF HEAVENS
OVER MY HEAD

Cello case in hand, I return to my seat. The fourth race has involved an objection-and-disqualification and horseplayers are wandering around in the vicinity of the cashiers' window shrieking and tearing at their hair or as the case might be, scalps: a distinctly unpleasant and odorous scene but so much hope in the air that you could cut it. Not only the people with tickets on the winning horse line up in front of the windows but the people with tickets on the horse which finished second; there is no question but that they have a chance to win as well and if so they will get an edge in. Thus there are two sets of winners warming up in front of the windows rather than the normal one but this is not purely a happy occasion because the winners hate one another and know that the existence of one will disprove the possibility of the other. It is, as I know from my own experiences in such circumstances, a very unpleasant and tense scene and it is no help to be part of it declaring that you cannot lose because you have tickets on both horses; every so often this will get one physically injured or at least close to that point. The only good thing about this scene, in fact, is that at least I am able to make my progress unnoticed: If Toscanini himself were to stride across the grandstand floor followed by the members of the NBC famous symphony orchestra, it would excite no comment at all even though Toscanini, that great conductor as we all know, has been dead for some fifteen years and most of the members of the NBC symphony are busy playing backgrounds for our best modern motion pictures. There is only one difficult moment, as a matter of fact, which occurs as I pass Julie's stand; I do not even realize for the instant that it is her stand and then recognize her. She is selling candy bars to a line of cursing horseplayers and as I pass her she gives me a long and calculating wink. "I haven't decided yet, I just want to think the whole thing over," I mouth to her hoping that she can lip-read and she winks at me, nods, says very loudly, "it's your decision, you do exactly what you feel is the best thing for you to do," causing the horseplayers to wheel and look at me with interest. I proceed toward the escalator, wondering if I am beginning to have some kind of a problem with relationships. It is discomfiting in the extreme to mouth something to someone who screams at you in return, leading you to the feeling that you are deaf or they aggressive. Also, the itching in the leg which I forgot about during my interview with the Winner has returned with what can be called a vengeance, and the very flesh of the thigh seems to be swelling, expanding underneath my touch. It is a very bad condition, in short, which seats me back in place in the grandstand and the sullen mood surrounding is no help either. The winner has been knocked down to fourth place and the second place horse to third. The third horse has won it, a rare double-disqualification, in short, and most of the horseplayers around me are not particularly pleased because the three was a forty to one shot. "The judges had a piece of that one, it was all maneuvered," horseplayers say to one another and express similar thoughts. I hunch myself over the cello case and try, at least momentarily, to remove myself from the situation and obtain a proper moment of rest, but as is usual at the racetrack, there is no rest at all. Three rows down from me a man goes berserk from the June heat or maybe only the double disqualification and stands, ripping off his shirt, clenching his fists, his face reddening in the sun as he screams, "come on, you sons of bitches, who wants to come with me! Who wants to tear that toteboard down!" He is a very vigorous, powerful man with good gestures and a fine voice but attracts only marginal interest. "You aren't going to stand for that are you?" he says, "how much of this are you supposed to take; do you want them to steal you out of everything?" and seizing a beer can which he must have smuggled in underneath his shirt, hurls it in the direction of the tote. The intent must have been wonderful, a scatter and a smash, but the wind catches it and it only sails lightly, daintily to the ground, wafting in the breeze. This problem or act of fate seems to set the man off completely. He mounts his seat and begins to jump up and down saying that the track announcer should drop dead and the races are all rigged, the horses being inhabited by men wearing horse-clothing who manipulate the races at their pleasure, none of it real, not even the odds. The whole thing is a dream put up by frauds, but at this accusation the powers that be at the racetrack seem to lose patience, finally. They have been tolerant up until now, and a number of Pinkertons appear from no point of origin and surround the man to take him away. He leaps sprawling on their shoulders and skillfully they render him unequal to dispute through certain physical maneuvers, then he is dragged out upside down, his hands flopping wearily, his eyes closed. The Pinkertons, I should point out, are a very reputable private detective agency who have been in the business of policing and protecting the New York tracks for several decades and all of them carry guns, meaning that it is somewhat unwise to make comments upon a Pinkerton's complexion or appearance. In his vanishing, the customer still seems to be heard, muttering about the devil that lives in the toteboard, but there is very little attention to be paid to this kind of thing once the immediate diversion is past, and along with the others, I sink back into my own stupor and contemplations. There is really very little to say about such incidents which happen by the score at Aqueduct Racetrack almost every day of the week and can be considered as part of the ritual. I do not mean to minimize the importance of the incidents or to sound unsympathetic but if one responded emotionally to every crazy person or incident which occurred at Aqueduct Racetrack during a given day, one would have no time to apply oneself to the horses which are, after all, the main business of this activity.

As I open the paper to gaze at the entries for the fifth, however, another thought hits me and it is one which makes me drop the paper and gaze out into space, once again abstracted and taken with complex thoughts. I do not care who wins the fifth in any event, sometime between the second race and my interview with the Winner a certain zeal seems to have been purged out of me. I have lost interest in the races or at least in my potential ability to deal with them and this leaves my mind free to deal with the single amazing thought which instantly takes over not the back but the forelobe of the brain and deserves a good deal of speculation. This thought is that even if Julie is telling the truth about the Counters and even if it is so that the Mob has been running things for several years, it was not that good before 1963 or years previous anyway. It simply was not that good.

It was not that good at anytime at all, when you come right down to it, it was downright bad. Racing in the days previous was even more corrupt than it is now, the film patrol and medical authorities having become more and more influential in recent years and also the rigging and manipulation of the races at the old Jamaica racetrack, particularly in the fall, had to be lost on to be believed. Also, there were the usual number of wars, deaths, pain and murder. There were just as many people suffering the pangs of what can be called social injustice, the only difference was that one was somewhat less conscious of it because one did not have the wonderful opportunities for sharing experiences that are available today.

These are deep thoughts, particularly deep for a one such as I who has never shown particular interest or ability for current events and who, along with most of my friends and acquaintances, has tried to avoid them. But the experiencing of them is quite strange; it is as if in some profound way I have never been truly thinking before this moment and if this is thought, I want no part of it. No less than the Chart or Harry the Flat I want easy answers or at least to believe in easy answers and the question of looking at the races from the sociological and political point of view is all a little bit too much for me. There is a limit to the kind of sensations and thoughts which one human being can take and certainly I have gone around that limit; nevertheless, the thoughts will not stop. Peculiar things are happening down on the track with one of the spraying trucks getting grounded near the toteboard and whole teams of men and trucks coming out to get it before it interrupts the proceedings for the fifth race, but this is only marginally interesting to me. It occurs to me that looking at the whole thing objectively, it might even be possible to say that things before 1963 were somewhat worse rather than better because one was not so close to the action and could take it seriously. It was in about 1963 that I overcame my naiveté toward the races, and came to understand what might possibly be going on there. This knowledge, at least, was something of a shield. If you knew they were out to get you, then you could at least handle yourself in prepared fashion, whereas, if you thought it was a clean honest sport, with equal chances for all horses, under the kind supervision of some expert stewards and commission people, you were in trouble from the start.

Too much, too much, particularly since the heat and the noise level in the grandstand seem to have risen from the times previous and it is very hard to hold thoughts in the head in such instances. People are shouting at one another and poking at the *Telegraph* with increasing ferocity, paying more attention to the stalled spraying truck at which they jeer and throw a few objects until finally a couple of Pinkertons circle out from the lower area and surround the machine. It is not easy to remain detached and composed within the area of the grandstand which is probably the reason why most systems, sooner or later, break down; the atmosphere of a fifth race is entirely different from that of a first.

Nevertheless, I am still trying to think, still struggling with the small compass of my thoughts when I am suddenly and perhaps permanently distracted. Leaning with chin on hand, watching them drag the machine away I am trying to remember my exact sensations during the time of change of governments, when there is a tap on my shoulder, an insistent, clammy tap which makes me turn around quickly and ready to strike anyone who would touch me in such a fashion. And then, looking at this person, see that I cannot strike them because this is the only person who might touch me that way.

Leaning over me, a crazy, twisted grin on her face, pain in her eyes, tension in the cords of her neck, is the lovely Gertrude nee Hawkins her hands still on my neck, the pages of a program flapping in one of them. She is wearing a very nice brown dress and looks very well-contained, indeed, except for her face. "Hello," she says, "I hoped I'd catch you here. I wanted to come. Aren't you glad to see me?"

Gertrude nee Hawkins until this moment has surely never been at a racetrack in her life. I sense that this is something of a manipulated job and behind that I sense something else, too, but this is the woman I love, this is the woman I care for, I rise and touch her, and guide her into the seat next to mine and only when her body sinks against me into the slats do I understand what kind of pain she has and now she must be suffering if her fine, rigid body collapses through my hands like the ooze of beer from a torn Stevens container.

XL

THE REACTION OF MY WIFE
TO THE ASSASSINATION
OF JOHN F. KENNEDY

"Never the same; it will never be the same again. It's one of those public events which happen once or twice in a lifetime which remind you that it's only a temporary universe and that the bottom can drop out of it at any time at all: don't you think that things are disintegrating? Can't you feel it somehow? It's just the most terrible thing that ever happened, will you take your eyes away from those goddamned entry sheets for one minute and listen to me?

"You can't run away from it all your life you know, sooner or later you have to come to terms with it and you'd better do it now. If this won't make you become responsible, what will, let me ask you? Our lives must change. We must understand that what has happened changes everything. What seemed possible before, isn't anymore. Can't you listen to me? Don't you want to hear any of this? Do you really think that there's any answer in the racing form?

"Yes, I guess you think there's an answer in the racing form. If you didn't think there was an answer you wouldn't be acting like this. People end up doing exactly what they want to do and I believe it, I believe you, I believe that you're doing exactly what you're meant to do. But I don't have to take it any more. There are going to be a whole lot of changes here whether you participate in them or not and that's all there is.

"I mean it's a terrible thing, almost a personal thing and if you ignore it you're missing the whole point of it. Public events *can* make a difference in our lives, in anyone's lives, look at the war. Look at the concentration camps. Do you think that just because something happens to people you don't know it has no effect upon you? You're wrong. You're entirely wrong.

"I see you won't listen to me so that's all right. I'm going to go out by myself, I have a lot of things to do. Maybe I'll be home tonight and maybe I won't. Maybe I'll see you and maybe I won't. Maybe we'll get together and maybe we won't. Everything must change. It cannot be the same.

"If I thought you thought that it would really make any difference in studying the racing form, I'd go along with you, but it really doesn't and you're smart enough to know that. You're not a stupid person. Most of the people who you're going to the track with, or who you meet out there, are very stupid, but you aren't. You ought to have more confidence in your intelligence. Just because you don't have all the education you thought you needed, is that a reason to destroy yourself?

"Why won't you listen to me? Why doesn't anything I say make any difference? It wasn't this way once; you listened to me for hours. We listened to each other. Don't you care? Don't you want to care? Is this exactly what you plan to do with the rest of your life?

"He's dead, dead, dead and nothing can change it but unless we become different because of this then it's all too pointless. Things must become different. Oh God, I can't stand to look at you any more."

XLI

THE POST THEORY OF HARRY THE FLAT

"The assistant starters, that's what you really got to watch. That's where most of the really crooked stuff goes on, right at the starting gate. "These assistant starters, they really know their business. They can do anything to a horse in there and no one would ever notice, twist a tail to make it quit, give them a kick in the knee so that they stiffen up or go sore, do something to their backs that makes them lose their action. I'm not saying that the jockeys aren't crooked as hell too but the jockeys wouldn't even know what's going on there, it all happens so fast. And after all of that, all they have to do is hold them back for a tenth of a second, make sure that the horse's door at the gate doesn't open for a split-second after the others do. A tenth of a second is half a length you know. You can knock an odds-on favorite out of a race before it's even started and who would know? Who could tell a tenth of a second, even on films? The stewards don't care, they get plenty of kickbacks for that nonsense.

"It's all rigged. The whole thing. You haven't got a chance and the funny thing is that all of this goes on right in front of the public and they couldn't even know the difference. They couldn't even tell. The thing to do is to make your bets after the start but that is not applicable in the state of New York, you must make your bets before the race. This is the way that they get you.

"There's no future. The whole thing is too rotten. It's all fixed and they can get you in a hundred different ways. But there's one advantage you got over them, they can't make you bet a horse. You pick the horse you want to bet and you bet him; they can't control that stuff. And that's why I say that it can still be beaten, although how you can beat it is beyond me.

"Let us look over these entries for the third. You will see that it is a maiden filly claimer which right away is impossible. You cannot beat these kind of races. Nobody can beat these kind of races. But I think I see a spot in this one if you will just move a little bit closer and maybe I can help you on some of the angles, if in turn, you can help me."

XLII

PUTTING IT TO GERTRUDE
NEE HAWKINS

"I came here to talk to you," she says when she is somewhat calmer and her breathing has returned to normal. "I wanted to see you so badly but I got lost coming off the train and went all the way to the other end of the grandstand and then climbed up and down three flights of stairs. I have to talk to you," she says and commences to pull herself two-handedly back in focus, tugging at her clothing, her hair, and so on. She is wearing a sleeveless brown dress and as she comes back into condition, begins once again, to remind me of the youthful and attractive woman who I have loved for such a long time. But there is also a distinctly ominous overcast which spoils the whole thing for me and also I do not like the fact that she has once again put on falsies to see me. This habit, which she cannot be broken of, indicates that she takes me for being consistently naïve or maybe only counting on the triumph of gullibility over memory. She has very nice and ample breasts and her attempts to move them up in class almost always result in disaster. "I want to talk to you," she says. "I came all the way here to talk."

"You told me that," I say, "and I know that you came here to talk because you simply did not come here to bet, that is one thing. Who sent you here? Did the Winner?"

"Where did you get that cello case?" she says, running a hand over it. "I never knew you played the cello, you never told me. Now my sister—"

"I do not play the cello," I say. "Tell me if the Winner sent you here."

"It's a wonderful instrument. Whenever I hear Picasso play it just knocks me straight out. I wish you did play."

"The man's name is Castles, Pablo Castles, not Picasso. Did the Winner send you here, Gertrude? What do you want?" This is, perhaps, not a very soothing way to talk to the woman you love but the point of this strange afternoon is, that I am not sure that I love her, as I have come to suspect the use of the word and also I do not like the Winner meddling in my private life, having seen the damage that he has already done with the Public. "What does the Winner want?"

"What a strange place," Gertrude says, looking from side to side, peering down at the stretch, looking up toward the eave of the grandstand, "it isn't at all like I thought it would be. It doesn't look anything like what you'd see in the movies. And it's all full of crazy people."

"Gertrude," I say and take her hand, not out of any sexual tendencies whatsoever but merely for emphasis; her hand is like iron in mine and the question of sexuality is impossible anyway, "Gertrude, I want you to talk to me directly because a number of things have happened to me this afternoon and I am somewhat reduced on time and patience. Also Gertrude, I am afraid that I am going to have to make an important decision soon which I am not really capable of making. You must come straight with me, Gertrude, I ask you this one favor and if you don't—"

"Oh," she says, withdrawing her hand and letting it fall to her lap, twitching her lap slightly, then leaning back so that I can get an excellent view of the false front which, like an odds-on choice, has no meaning at all to me, "oh you have no consideration at all, where's your sensitivity? I come all the way out to see you and I get lost and I run up and down three flights and finally find you—"

"How did you find me? How did you know where I was, Gertrude?"

And at this line satisfactory results emerge; she crumples as if a rein had been yanked cruelly into her mouth and folds in upon herself on the seat shaking her head, putting her fists against her eyes, "oh God," she says, "oh God, all right, have it your way, just have it your way. Please do it, that's all I want to say, please do it."

"Do what?"

"He hurt me, I can't take this anymore, he came out to my house and he said I had to get down and make you do it. And I said I didn't have any contact with you that way and never even saw you at the races and didn't see how I could make you do anything. Then he told me what they had done to you and then he hit me and said that he would do the same thing to me. Oh for God's sake, do what he wants, will you? It's the only way out and I can't take it anymore."

"Ah," I say, "ah," leaning back into my seat with a real sense of revelation; it is not pleasant news to hear that my paramour or ex-paramour has been assaulted by Tony Winner but on the other hand, it reconstitutes my shrinking faith in an orderly, motivated universe and this is all to the good. "And he sent you out here," I say, "sent you out to persuade me. So how are you supposed to persuade me, Gertrude?"

"Oh I don't care," she says, flinging her face back from her fists and staring straight out toward the tote, "I don't care anymore, I think that all of you are crazy and I can't stand it. When the Flat died I should have left the state. Why the hell I had to stick around and get involved with a friend of his I don't know. Maybe it was guilt, because I thought that somehow I was to blame and if I couldn't make it for the poor Flat I could do something for a friend of his. But I was wrong, all wrong. He's a terrible man and he's going to hurt you very badly unless you do this. I don't know how to persuade you, he said that I would find a way. All of you people are crazy! Don't you think about anything except attacking one another? Where are your hearts?"

"It works two ways, Gertrude," I say, thinking of certain tendencies which she herself has been known to show time and again. Her revelation has given me the most wonderful sense of detachment, and suddenly (this has never happened before), I feel on top of the situation, "it works two ways but he really shouldn't have made you come, there really wasn't any point or purpose in that kind of thing. The Winner should know better."

"So what do you care?" she shrieks, "what do you care that I think enough about you to come out and try to beg you to do something for your own sake. For God's sake, if you have to do it, just go ahead and do it. I don't care what he wants, do you want to be killed or not?"

"Do you know what I'm supposed to do, Gertrude?"

"Well no," she says, "no, he didn't exactly tell me that. I know that it has something to do with Harry but I don't really care. That wasn't important to him, telling me I mean, all that he wanted to get over to me was that I was supposed to make sure you followed through. So I'm trying! I'm trying! I don't even *like* you anymore!"

"That's not the point, Gertrude," I say and take her hand gently, wondering how I can best put this so that we will remain on the best of terms and yet avoid further emotional complications, "the point is that he really should have told you, although, I grant you that up until now it was supposed to be a surprise. Do you know what I am supposed to do? Listen Gertrude, I better tell you, it's only fair. The Flat is under the backstretch there, he's been there for almost four years. Contrary to the information you were given, he did not fling himself off a bridge into undiscovered waters but instead shot himself on the spot and was carried to a resting place later by his friends and acquaintances. His presence on the backstretch, however, has been lousing up the Mob's figures something terrible, and it has now been decided that the time has come to get him out. The Flat, therefore, was to be removed by me after the eighth race this afternoon—what remains of him that is, so that the backstretch could be smoothed and the figures would stand up. It was the intention of those interests with whom I was dealing to present you with the Flat's remains, very tastefully of course, in a covered box, so that you would have something sentimental to remember him by, but things have now run into complications having nothing to do with the Flat. But the real thing is that the Winner should have told you this. It would have been the decent thing to do, since you are so well-acquainted with the deceased, even to this date."

To her credit, she takes all of this very well, her eyes turning progressively blank as she listens, but otherwise her responses very good, within the normal range as we say, although toward the end she gags slightly. When I am finished I poise myself for any kind of response but she says nothing for an instant and so I say, "did you hear me? Is it all right?"

"Crazy," she says with that fine Catholic finality which has to me always been one of the least attractive sectors of Gertrude nee Hawkins. "Crazy. All of you people are insane. I knew I should never have gotten involved with any of you. But I was trying to hold onto options. You're all totally insane." "You haven't heard nothing of it yet," I say. Our discussion has, incidentally, attracted some down on the track. The horses break from the looks of intensity I am receiving, it occurs to me that possibly I have been talking too loudly. "Forget it," I say, "everything will be all right," hoping that the listeners will take it as a lover's quarrel. "Meanwhile," I say, "let us watch the fifth, which is just beginning," and so it is right down on the track. The horses break from the gate and run from the six furlong mark through the homestretch and onto the finish wire while around us people scream and curse and pray and throw things. Seated in the middle of this activity, observing the penitential form of Gertrude Hawkins, holding one of her cold hands calmly I feel quite detached from all of it. It is strange that people would generate such emotions toward horses. It is strange that they would carry on so over something so repetitious and dull. It is madness to think that this can be taken seriously. It is impossible to believe that it makes any difference.

XLIII

PREMONITIONS OF THE DEMISE
OF HARRY THE FLAT

Harry the Flat's regrettable suicide was not entirely unforeshadowed although it was, for this reason, none the less tragic, of course. Often in the depths of a losing streak the Flat would say things like "I ought to blow my brains out if this keeps up" or "what the hell's the use if this is all it comes to?" and so on, but most of his complaints were taken for the routine lament of the horseplayer. When the Flat would enter a winning streak or an even period they would disappear so completely that friends and acquaintances felt justified in their belief that the Flat was only posturing. Besides, they had their own problems.

Still, it would have been possible to have noted through a careful observation of the Flat that his remonstrances and predictions might have been taken more seriously than otherwise posted. In periods of repose, a slack kind of terror would creep into the corners of his face, moving from the mouth through the cheeks and then to the eyes, the eyes stunned in the center of these panels winking for light, a tremor of the forehead for concentration taking on the aspect of a tic. At times a heavy sigh would overtake the Flat, this sigh being seemingly unrelated to extrinsic events and wrenching his body throughout; causing him to tremble as if ill.

"Someday I'm gonna get a gun and plug someone," the Flat would say, "plug them straight through the head for doing all this that they done to me, I'll get them for this, I'll get them," and who of us was to know, who of us would have suspected, who of us would have possibly apprehended that the person the Flat would get was himself? so neatly and finally in the grandstand, the tissue of his brains in the explosion floating like a halo around his beaten, honest head, the astonishment of the moment seen only in his mouth which pursing toward an O dropped toward extinction as gun in hand he dropped to our feet, kneeward, praying.

XLIV

HOW IT ALL WENT AWAY

Looking at Gertrude nee Hawkins then, the fifth race over and in the bag and who the hell knows or cares what has happened? Looking at her I see what she is, as if for the first time: she is a thirty-five year old woman, maybe thirty-six, beginning to crumble slightly around the edges, held in toward the center by bone and conviction, but now in the extremity of the moment, some of this seems to have given out, and coming from the sides of her I can see something weak, soft and horrifying. I can see what she will look like in ten years or maybe less when the interest goes away, and seeing her in that fashion I understand that I am in love with her no longer. It is a regretful insight since I am, basically, a loving person looking only for things I can trust and cherish. But it is better sooner than never, or so I think, and in any event there is something about the way she holds her body that frightens me. There is an edge to the arch that tells me of many things and all of them are losers. "Oh do it," she is saying, "oh just do it anyway, what do I care, just listen to them, what else can you do? They're crazy, they're crazy. But don't you bring that thing to me, I'll kill you if you bring me anything like that."

"I doubt that there is anything left," I say, "he would only be ashes and decomposition by now. I do not think that there would even be any question of a smell to annoy you."

"*Oh*," she says and springs against the seat, then stands, shuttling the program under her arm, "oh, I just can't talk to you, I just can't stand to listen to this anymore. I've got to get out of here, just do it, listen to me, if that's what they want, do it. Do it." She is, I manage to surmise then, very much afraid of the Winner and who, in her circumstances, would not be? "I don't want to see you anymore," she says, "I think you're crazy."

"It's a crazy business," I say and stand. A strange courtliness seems to take me over; what I want to do is usher Gertrude out of the grandstand with style. If there is no feeling left, then certainly style must make up the difference, and it is suddenly very important that the matter be accomplished gracefully. "I'm sorry," I say, "I mean I'm sorry that you had to get involved with this. Did he take you over?"

"This horrible *man* came and took me over. And now I'm leaving. I don't think I want to see you anymore."

"I understand that," I say, "I mean I know that you could get around to having this point of view. But it's nothing personal."

"I don't know how you people *think*. I don't even know what you have in mind, how your mind works." She sways against me, I support her, I lead her toward the door. Some horseplayers are looking at us with interest but most are not. It is something that happens all the time; many marriages, let alone affairs, have broken up in the grandstand. "I just don't even understand," she says girlishly, never so much confusion in the voice of Gertrude Hawkins and I hold onto her, she leans against me, I escort her to the mouth of the exit and say, "well, I guess I'll see you around. Later, or something like that."

"See me around? You mean you're going to just send me away like this? You're not even going to take me out of this foul place?"

"Let us be logical, Gertrude," I say, "if I escort you home or even part of the way then I will never be back here in time to accomplish my appointed tasks and it is exactly those tasks which you were delegated to send me out to persuade what with to do."

"You're not talking straight. I don't follow you."

"You cannot both ways it have done, Gertrude," I say, finding this manner of talking suddenly very refreshing and kiss her gently right on the steps, horseplayers scuttling to the sides of us, then push her gently on her way. "Be reasonable," I say, being prepared for anything, "be reasonable," and she leaves me without another word, holding her shoulders straight, moving into the mob. From the rear she looks like any lady horseplayer. I watch my lost love depart, sunken in the surprising knowledge that I feel absolutely nothing for her and then, in the midst of all this temporary triumph and satisfaction I remember that I have left the goddamned cello case back at the seat.

I rush back and it is still there, although slightly dishevelled. One corner peeks open and I can see the outlines of the implements. A horseplayer, perhaps, wished to comfort himself with some music after a loss but finding to his dissatisfaction that not music but excavation lay within, abandoned it all to go on his own way, perhaps interpreting the presence of the cello as a musical tip, perhaps, on the basis of its elements, deciding against music forever. It is hard to say, either way it will work out in the same fashion. I sit down and open the *Telegraph* looking at the sixth race entries—how quickly and interestingly this afternoon has gone—but being overcome soon enough by boredom, put it away. Scuttling in the rear of my mind like a small animal is the impetus of an idea; I think that I know finally what I am going to do and the sensation of verging upon epiphany is enormous, I can contend with it only by clutching my fists, squeezing my eyes closed and trying to think of neutral things. Horseplayers burble, cogitate, moan to one another; after a while I get up and taking the cello with me I leave my seat yet once again and head toward the nearest men's room. It seems a good enough place to think and I have had the majority of my most original thoughts in circumstances like these.

XLV

THE FLAT DEMOLISHED

Rolling on the ground, the gun falling from his fingers, his head draining, his eyes open one last time and catch mine, I bend over him, looking into his face and it is surprising, for all the damage inflicted, how calm and knowledgeable those eyes are. Now that pain and implosion having taken his life away, it is as if the interior of the Flat can return to a central peace. The eyes flicker, then fixate, he seems to be at rest and in a kind of control which he has not managed for a long time. "Come here," he mutters, crooking a finger and I kneel beside him, a rare honor, the last of the Flat's associates to talk to him ever, "You understand," he mutters, licking his lips, "you understand that there was a whole different way of doing things which I never wanted to take. You don't think that any of this was easy, do you? It had to be this way, bury me on the backstretch so that at least I can feel them running over me when I'm in heaven," and expires with a Calvinist shudder, his hands opening. The death-speech of the Flat, the sincerity of his conviction that after all is done he will yet go to heaven, the brutal shock of the entire instance most disconcerts me and it is difficult to keep the tears from my eyes as I look upward. "He died happy," I inform those surrounding, "he died happy and it is his last wish to be buried where the horses run." Snuffles come from above, and Tony Winner who is not the Winner then but merely a small, hounded guy named Tony Nickels who has dedicated himself to learning everything that the Flat can teach him, nods slowly and says, "if that's what the Flat wants, that's what he gets. It would be an honor to do this thing for my great friend the Flat," and then turns to the others saying, "anybody going to stop me? Anybody say that the Flat can't get his last will and testament?" and because Tony Nickels then and now is a very forceful guy (although then he had somewhat less substance of course) nobody says a word of protest, there are only assenting nods. "I will do this thing for the Flat," Nickels says, "because he is a truly great man, and a little bit of bad luck at the very end does not mean that he is any less great. I will meet his needs because he is entitled to that." I stand, somewhat shakily, and Nickels put an arm around me. "This man and I will be responsible for seeing that the Flat's news and views never die," he says, "but remain and go on and on, isn't that right? Isn't that right?" I assure him that it is. Tony Nickels soon enough catches on to the right connections and begins to move upward and onward very rapidly; takes advantage of certain political events in the Mob to improve his career and unfortunately forgets most of what he vowed but underneath he remains the same strong, simple person, I tell myself, and can be counted on in a pinch. Only later and in unpleasant circumstances do I learn that this is not so but by then the Flat, in the Winner's calculations, is already half dug-up and Gertrude sent on the heartstring detail to keep me in the service of the Plan.

XLVI

THE FLAT'S BASIC DICTA ON HORSEPLAYING

1. Never bet fillies against mares or female horses of any kind against colts or geldings. Never bet a horse moving up more than one thousand dollars in class from his race unless he won that last race easily or lost it in an effort which did not tax him. Never bet a horse dropping down in class unless he ran badly in his last race in which case bet him if he is the only such animal in the field and has a claiming value of at least three thousand dollars less than the highest price at which he has ever run.

2. Never bet a horse of more than eight to one on the board unless there are at least six such horses in a race, in which case, bet each of them to win and place and parlay after every loss. Never bet a horse who goes off at less than eight to five unless you are playing full progression in which case bet him to show only and triple the ordinary bet. These are the basic mathematical systems embraced by the System of Rules Conservation, although advanced horseplayers may find one which is even more satisfactory to them.

3. Never bet a horse ridden by an apprentice jockey unless the apprentice is: a) one of the leading apprentices at the meeting and b) has ridden the horse before and c) is getting the horse a weight advantage of three pounds minimum over the rest of the field and d) has not ridden the horse before and e) is one of the less well-known apprentice jockeys at the plant indicating that the trainer and owner are trying to put something over by getting a price and f) has not had any disqualifications, objections or suspensions within the last thirty days.

4. In two year old maiden sprints always bet the horse which has the best previous time at the distance unless there is in the race a first-time starter who has worked out to within one second of this horse's time. In which case bet the first-time starter unless he comes from a minor stable or is out of a routing sire or is ridden by a jockey who has not won at least ten percent of his races at the meeting or trained by a trainer who has won ten percent. In which case, the bet on the previously-raced horse should be increased times the amount of fifths of seconds under which his best previous time is underneath the average track record for the distance on that day allowing a three times credit if the jockey is a national or local leader or if the trainer has in the past produced a series of betting coups. Make no allowance for mudders, routers, or horses which seem to run best on a firm but holding track.

5. Rainy day system: give two points to every horse in the race which has previously run in the slop and three points to every horse who has not, unless the ones who have not have shown some inclination to run at minor tracks

whose track variants are fifteen percent lower than major track variants. In which case they should be given four points credit and calculated on the problematical percentage play. Of those horses which have the lowest point total, allow the geldings extra credit and bet them to win and place. Of those horses who have the higher point total give fillies extra credit and bet them to place and show as a longshot system. If this requires that every horse in the race be bet, eliminate one and bet the others unless the one eliminated has a low point credit; in which case, double the bet on this one and remain at the single unit with the other.

6. Try to leave after the sixth race, the subways become very unpleasant after the feature race and it is bad enough to ride home a loser without having to do it without a seat. Think of dignity, live in dignity, and try to cultivate some sense of self-respect.

XLVII

IN THE MEN'S ROOM: AN ASSAULT
OF COLOR

Into the men's room on the third level of the Aqueduct grandstand. Aqueduct is short on atmosphere, a place of difficulty for many other reasons, but one thing it has never lacked is men's rooms, running three or four apiece to the grandstand and clubhouse, large and roomy places which may be the safest and most efficient public rest rooms in North America, a place to which you could send your son with pride and security. Moving there, the cello case now under my arm in a professional fit, I pass Julie's stand, mean to pass her a comforting meaningless wink to keep her content during my Moment of Decision but the stand is closed, boarded on all sides, a sign hanging off-kilter from the wall which says CLOSED FOR THE SEASONAL, WE THANKS YOU FOR YOUR PATRONAGE. Three or four chewing gum wrappers and cigarette packs crumpled in the vicinity are the only testimony that this was, until so recently, a successful, prospering division of the Harry M. Stevens concession belt. Nostalgia would be an insane emotion to entertain under these circumstances and yet, looking at the abandoned stand I feel nothing else: this was where I was told about the Counters, this was where Julie and I established a special and permanent relationship and relationships of whatever sort are not to be discounted in the brutal and interesting world of Aqueduct Racetrack. The fact that the sign seems to be rather poorly phrased also bothers me a trifle: one would wonder what to make of an organization which wants to rule the world, yet has members that are not particularly strong on the language. Despite the fact that I lack extensive education and do not associate with a class of people who worship the spoken word, I have always tried to cultivate a certain elegance of speech myself as being one of those things which truly separate the men from the beasts. I would not like to think of a world run by people who now and then close things up for the season. Still, this is extraneous thinking, not really applicable to the situation and I decide that I will discard it out of hand. I come into the men's room, walk past the urinals and join a shifting, pale line of men waiting for cubicles in front of a white-coated attendant. Most of the men look uncomfortable in the extreme but it is not diarrhea which seems to afflict them so much as constipation; a look of dark blockage, a suggestion in their faces that they know they are committed to try their bowels as their luck, but in both cases, very little will happen. The attendant, who I have known off and on for several years although never in a non-professional capacity winks at me and shouts down the line, "a booth. One booth coming up for the cellist!" and the others look at me with some anger while I shift the case to the other arm and try to look as normal as possible. The policy is for the attendants to call up and down the line, setting up vacancies for the customers and keeping matters regularized but there is something about the presence of a cello case on line which convinces some of the customers that they are once again being manipulated and there are some mumbles and mutters. "No problem," I say, taking out a handkerchief, and wiping off my face with a bit of residue from the grandstand. "No problem at all, everything's fine," and they look away grunting, having concluded perhaps, that I am somewhat mentally unstable. This is a judgment to which they would be entitled. In their places I would feel the same way.

It is hot in this bathroom, terribly hot, even worse here than in the under-grandstand itself because of the compression and bodily acts which are being performed but it seems to bother few of the horseplayers. Not one of whom seems to be even on the verge of fainting. At the urinals men stand holding themselves with one hand and their newspapers with the other. Selections seem to mingle with urine and there is an absence of the harsh whistling and clatter which seems to be the understanding of most public rest rooms and locker rooms. Now and then someone will get an insight in the act of elimination which insight will cause him to forget to close his clothing after finishing. But the attendants are kind about this and never miss the opportunity to remind. Due to the diligence of horseplayers and the conscientious work of these attendants there has not been a single case of indecent exposure at Aqueduct in its entire eleven year history, a record which is duplicated as far as I know by no other public facility.

Some time has passed while I indulge myself with these homey, men's rooms reflections and I am now the first on line, the attendant leans over and asks me if I have anything good for the day and how I have done so far. I give him fifty cents, the normal cubicle tip, and say that the day has not been too interesting and that as far as I know I have nothing for the rest of the day; I may, in fact, even leave early.

"Don't do that," he says, "you'll feel much better after you've taken care of yourself here. Listen, I got something for you. It's been coming in all afternoon and I'm glad to let you have it. I been hearing it so much I'm going to bet that bugger myself in the eighth race."

"The eighth?"

"Sure thing. Knockover. That dog is gonna be thirty, forty to one on the board and there's a lot of inside money working on the horse. Maybe bet down to ten to one with all the tips floating around but any price is a good price if you win and that horse is set up. I'm going to bet him ten and ten and I ain't even a serious bettor. I'd get on him if I were you."

"I've heard a few things about him," I say, "I guess there's some word out."

"Word out, why man, I been hearing that one all day. They've been talking up Knockover since I came on shift at eleven this morning, which you must agree is a hell of a long time to stand in a men's room shuttling folks around, seven hours without a break and my feet hurt. One for the cellist?" "One for the cellist!" the man way down calls cheerfully and I insert a hand in a pocket, find another fifty-cents, pass it on to my friend and still trundling the case walk down the long line of closed cubicles feeling vaguely as if I were making entrance before the assembled orchestra at Carnegie Hall. "Hey, I'll hold that," the other attendant says as I make my way into a fine, small booth, "no need to go in with that thing," but I wave him off, hearing him mumble something obscene and close the door on him, bolt it and then cleverly use a second hidden bolt at the top to protect my safety. The presence of the second bolt is known only to Harry M. Stevens concession rest room employees but one picks up certain pieces of information after having been at the track for a long time, this is part of the acculturation process or in any event has to do with the process of socialization. With the door inevitably bolted on me now, with no possibility whatsoever of being intercepted in my difficult meditations I do something complex and yet at the same time quite simple, I fold my hands, lean my forehead on them and try to think things out calmly, coolly, rationally, paying as little heed as possible to the disparate goings on beyond the booth.

It is strange, strange to reduce all of the difficult and surprising events of this day to a series of reflections which I can work through in an orderly fashion in a men's room but I have no choice, I need to think now and the men's room is as good an enclosure as the track offers, the clubhouse restaurant to the contrary, the important thing is to return to the elements, so to speak, from whence one came and so sitting that way, fully clothed, upon Harry M. Stevens toilet bowl I work things through my mind as best I can while turning off the murmur outside. From the groans and sighs to the right and left of me one would think that horseplayers were seeking winners in the bathroom as assiduously as release, every now and then a sigh is broken by a small *ah!* of discovery and it is impossible to tell whether it is the bowels or the entry forms which have opened up. Certainly, if all the knowledge which seems to be in the process of revelation in this bathroom were converted into actual results, things would be entirely changed. Or then again, things might come out entirely the same. The question of picking winners, it has been noted, is a highly individualized process.

All of it works its way through what passes tentatively for my mind: Gertrude, the Winner, reminiscences of the Flat, Julie, Needles, the Chart, my own reasons for being here, my own background and history and now as I give myself over to it fully I find that it is literally too much; too much experience for my ability to absorb and shaking my head I retreat, back off it and try to take things item by item, picking them up and inspecting each separately

before going on to the next. It is difficult to order all of these factors: to explain a world which can contain both the Chart and the Flat for instance, or
Gertrude and myself, but I try, I do, as always, the best I can and I hear small
groans and murmurs escaping me no less than my unclothed seatmates, it is
difficult, it is so difficult, but I push further into the center of it persuaded that
if I think sufficiently all of it will come clear.

And then there occurs to me one of those remarkable moments known only
to characters in books and unlike anything which has ever happened to me
before, something going contrary to everything I believe I have come to
learn about the way the human mind and human affairs work, something so
interesting and enormous that I know it will change my whole life thereafter.
For what comes over me in the Harry M. Stevens men's room in the middle
of all my struggling efforts to think is nothing less than a sudden and complete insight, a whole total insight which explains everything and orders it
completely and although this is something which I myself can hardly believe,
having grown accustomed to photo-finishes, the eighteen percent takeout and
the process of disqualification, I seize onto it, choosing to believe that if it happens one must go no further. I grab onto the insight grunting, poise it between
my hands, shift it so to speak from one hand to the other, bounce it in the air,
my eyes widening with wonder and still it holds, the more I toss it, the longer
it stays and it holds together, it holds together. It is, as the expression goes,
nothing less than an entire epiphany, a word that I picked up in the course of
my travels but which I have never previously had sufficient cause to use. This
is the occasion. An epiphany. I have had an epiphany.

It ties everything together: the Winner, the Mob, the Counters, the Chart,
lesser functionaries like Gertrude or myself, it even begins to verge upon a true
and final explanation of the races and the way in which they are run. If
pushed to even the slightest degree this theory might well tell, for all I know,
how to pick winners, but my aims are far beyond greed and I do not explore
it in that direction. Instead, I only stay in the center, looking at the lovely and
more immediate applications.

"Oh God," I find myself murmuring, "oh God, it's too much, too much,"
and the attendant, always concerned or at least alert, pounds on the door to
ask me if I am feeling all right. I tell him that I am and try to settle lower on
the seat. "Too much, too much," I murmur and then, as I pass through it and
to the other side the final part of it hits me and I see not only the explanation
but the action. I see exactly what I must do. I see how everything can be followed upon to produce a resolution as clear and sparkling as the water on the
infield lake must have been a long time ago before Aqueduct Racetrack in the
borough of Queens came to grow up around it.

Naturally I cannot reveal the insight. This would not be fair and would also
be a violation of the principle of etiquette at the racetrack which holds that if

the other man paid seventy-five cents for his Lawton and you have no Lawton because you did not care to invest that money, you do not, in crowded quarters, seize the sheet from the man's hand and make his selections your own through greed and irresponsibility. There is a certain tacit understanding at the track and this is perhaps the only part of its grace, this tacit understanding being that you get exactly what you pay for, you work things through precisely on your own and what the other man has purchased in knowledge you do not seize from him because you must get it only in your own way and through as hard or easy a process as this turns out to be. Only the results are to be shared and communicated, but they come far after the fact. After the fact. After the fact. Everything is after the fact. Groaning, I hoist myself from the seat, grunting, I seize my cello case and then, loosening the bolts slowly, I edge my way out into the larger circumstance of the men's room and therefrom to perform my final and summary mission.

XLVIII

THE SUMMATION OF HARRY THE FLAT

"It comes to nothing, absolutely nothing. You cannot beat it. The only ones who beat it are the big-edge guys, those who are behind the whole operation and rig the results, but the guy going out there day by day simply has no chance. This guy going out to play them off the newspapers and his best judgment has got to lose because it's all rigged against him. The only way to understand the races is through information and there just is no information for those who are outside because that would kill the whole game. It's an insider's pastime and they're making millions off of us by using us to be there and put the money into the wrong selections.

"There is just no way that you can beat it because it really makes no sense. It just makes enough sense, a tiny little bit on the edges, to give you the feeling once in a while, that you're stupid and if you could only see things the way they were supposed to be seen you would have a chance but they put that in just for the figures. That's the only reason. Mainly it makes no sense at all and the fact that favorites win one-third of the time year after year, track after track, is only part of the whole arrangement that they make so that it turns out looking systematic.

"I have dedicated my whole like to understanding them and now I see that I was a fool, that they made a fool out of me, that there is nothing, nothing, and no way could I have ever beaten it unless I wanted to start at the bottom of whatever organization it is and pick up a little piece of information here and there as I moved along. That was the only way but I didn't do it; I thought that you could study and prepare yourself at the races just like you could for any other thing and that you could make an education of it but I was wrong.

"I was wrong about everything, I was played for a fool and now I can't stand it anymore. It just doesn't seem to be worth it to you if something you spent your whole life learning blows up in your face and it turns out that you should have been trying something else entirely with your time. At least if I was a failure going into business I would be making some money, less than I should be but there would be something in it for me. But this is ridiculous. This part of it is ridiculous. I'm losing money all the time; I'm a guy who goes into the office at twelve every day and doesn't come home until ten at night and stays up all night working and I'm losing money. It cost me money to work. I can't stand it no more.

"No more, no more, I can't stand it: I thought that I saw a system but I was all wrong. But the only thing, the thing that I can't understand, the thing that I got to live with somehow if I want to live, the thing that I never took into account is how beautiful the whole thing was. How beautiful.

"Why did it have to be that way? Why did it have to be so beautiful? That was what made all of the trouble, after that I never had a chance."

XLIX

THE HORSES ARE ON THE TRACK.
IT IS NOW POST-TIME

The sixth race. Or perhaps the seventh. it might even be the eighth coming up after all, it is impossible to know exactly how long I was in the men's room. Nor do I care. Pushing through the clumps of men staggering in in small groups I conclude that a race must have just finished; they are talking to one another in high desperate tones, already tearing at their clothing to expose themselves and void fully of the happenings. I give the attendant at the far end fifty cents thanking him for the services of his clean concession and then move into the undergrandstand for the last time. I know it is the last time because nothing I now see bothers me. One can take everything if it is the last time.

None of it bothers me at all; not the heat, the congestion, the sense of the entrapment, the rush of the crowds, the high bleat which seems to have no source but congeals from all of the voices, the ashen flicker of the tote, the clink of glasses from Harry M. Stevens bars, the sound of coffee burbling from the Harry M. Stevens grandstand refreshment counters. None of it has any effect upon me at all because there has been an added starter in this race and the added starter is that I know for me this is the last time. There will be nothing beyond this, all things coming to an end sooner or later in the run of things. Now, looking at it from the vantage point of one spending his last moments there all of it seems to have retreated from its ghastly high proportions, reduced, contained, it has the look of a series of artifacts strewn over the spaces of this vanished racetrack and I spring toward the light and exit of the doors, case bouncing on my back. Some elements of my fine coherency seem to have been lost, but on the other hand I seem to be feeling better, considerably better, at an entirely different vantage point. At the doors I pause only briefly, surrounded by *Telegraph*-reading men right and left, balance myself on the heels, undo the cello case in a series of rapid snaps and zippers and pull from it the spade and shovel, fine, dense, black instruments, not terribly differentiated but still distinct in my mind, there is a *spade* and there is a *shovel* and both of them are for the glory of the Flat. Horseplayers look at me blinking. "I've got business to do," I say, "excuse me please," and hurl the case down the lawn, it bounces off someone's head and then lands in a small, grey, open space, rolls once and is still. Very similar to the graceful dying motions of the Flat. "Important business, important business," I say, lifting the implements above my head and people give me headway, people definitely form an alley for me—how simple all of this is once you cultivate just a little bit of perspective—and I walk down the alley singing, waving my implements, fixating my gaze on the backstretch which is being tilled by one of the wary but loyal NYRA racing trucks, putting the strip into shape again for yet another race, courtesy of the track maintenance department to say nothing of the Government of the State of New York which allows all of this to be run and run again, six afternoons in all the seasons, at only the most minimal percentage of the take. It is good of the State of New York to allow this thing to be done; it shows that as always the Empire State is thinking of its citizens. Down the infield lawn I go singing and waving my instruments, conducting what I feel to be an imaginary fugue as I cut down the alley of horseplayers and approach the gate which separates grandstand from paddock and then paddock from track, the gate manned by a young Pinkerton who looks at me without surprise or interest as I close, for his sake, a hell of a lot of ground. "Coming through, coming through," I chant madly and they let me through, the instruments trailing after me, their glances awed and respectful because of all the people at the track at this moment only I, or have I got this wrong, seem to be doing something meaningful. "Coming through, coming through," thinking how proud the Flat would be of me at this moment, I having accepted the Flat's fourth and fifth lower dictums of the racetrack which state that precipitate action is the best to take when in doubt. Lights flicker on the tote, another odds drop, the four horse appears to be the money what with going down from two to one to eight to five. More maneuvering. More manipulation out of the paddock and the clubhouse for the racing fans to think about. The hell with them. I approach the gate, fling a hand within, use a delicate cellist's grasp to spring the latch and move into the paddock. I have never been in the paddock before and it is something of a thrill to be in this place where only horses, employees and the gentry walk. The air seems less congealed, thinner, higher, truer, one could spend a whole lifetime or at least a good part of it calculating the beneficial aspects of paddock air which is why a long time ago I thought that I wanted to own a horse. But there is neither time nor need for appreciation. "Excuse me," I say to the Pinkerton and walk with monstrous, perfect casualness through the gate, "I have something to do on the backstretch." The Pinkerton, who appears to be about twenty-four years of age with what Gertrude would call cuttingly (this is one of her many deficiencies as a woman, her cruelty) a "social problem" gives me one look of astonishment, a twitch which rolls his eyes back into his head and makes a tentative motion to stop me. "You can't do that," he says, "you can't go out on the track," and I confront him full by the eyes, take him figuratively by the scruff of the neck and say, "listen, let me alone. Let me go. You don't like this anymore than I do, do you?" and let him think about that for a moment while I stroll onto the track, the dirt shifting a little bit under my shoes. The guard is indeed thinking about this, one can see him thinking, the calculations twitching through his head, perhaps he is thinking about all the missed tips that have floated by him in this area, perhaps of all the owner's wives and daughters who in their sleeveless summer dresses have wafted past him as if he did not exist which in any sense they understand is correct. Maybe he is thinking of curses which come down on him from all the heights of the grandstand when something happens that they think they do not like and maybe when all is said and done, maybe he is thinking of nothing at all except how little he cares about the situation and how much he doubts his effect upon it, a common racetrack problem, because for whatever reason he lets me through. He does not follow me. He gives me a gesture which although vaguely obscene obviously signifies respect and dismissal and is awkward only because of his own lack of social grace.

Now, on the track I feel the place where the horses run: it is nothing like I imagined it at all, neither firm nor corporeal but a strange, shifting blend of sand and mud which seems to wobble underneath my shoes as I trudge toward the rail and then, along the rail, toward the backstretch. Saving ground all the way. It is possible that I am attracting attention, certainly there appears to be a sequence of noises behind me, cheers and mumbles, groans and threats, interesting that they would respond to such an ordinary act in such a way. A man going to do a routine gardening job. A man bringing the mechanical tools of disinterment to a simple task. Holding the rail through the clubhouse turn, I continue on my way, looking at the ground for the most part, staring now and again at the sky which shows more horizon from this perspective than one generally finds in New York City. Two astonished swans regard me from a distance and then paddle in the opposite direction. I salute them, these silent witnesses of more struggle than any of us have ever known and continue on my way. The spade and shovel clatter against one another. The crowd moves into the background. There is a strange bucolic peace to all of this, conducted under a hot sun and on turf that feels like loam. Strangeness, strangeness. I pass the starting gate which for the next race has been pulled all the way into the chute, two furlongs behind the necessary six-furlong marker. Man and horses are around the gate but they are at a far distance and make no move toward me; small figures, a quarter of a mile into abstraction they take my salute as I pass and similarly make no move towards me. I believe that I am going to get away with it. At the present moment, everything seems to be surprisingly in control, even my own respiration and heartbeat which continue at a moderate level. Only small spouts of beer curling within me near the belt-line remind me that I have a digestive system at all. I take the turn slowly, slowly, reminding myself that it is around this very turn that some of the greatest and worst horses in history have campaigned: the mighty Kelso used to ease up here after his winning races; here too Branch and Filatonga, two of my all-time favorites used to begin that series of quitting gestures which had such magnificent causes in the backstretch;

here Buckpasser would make his positioning movements and Brush Baron begin to bear out, here Priceless Gem would nail down a firm three-length lead and here Coachlight Square would begin to show nothing in mile and an eighth starter handicaps. Too much, too much for the likes of me and I begin to feel like a monument myself as I trudge toward the six-furlong pole. This part, at least, is all mapped out for me. I do not need to do research. I can see the place where Harry lies quite clearly; it glitters faintly in the sun and small insects seem to squirm into the turf as I approach.

Looking at the grandstand from this vast distance I can see what jockeys are talking about, can begin to understand why, even when everything is known about it, one might still want to race and race; move the horses out of this isolation into that distant bulk which sits and glints half a mile away. Now it is very quiet, only the shift of color denoting humanity, the glaze of prisms suggesting pain. It is very beautiful. There are a few forms running at me across the infield but they are a great distance away and at least in this perspective, appear to be in no hurry. I begin to dig.

Simple, simple, spade into the ground, lurch, grunt, shove, dirt flying, shovel discarded to one side since only the one implement was needed, the overly-protective Winner wrongfully insisting upon two. The shovel splits the ground neatly, halving it like the center of an apple, excavation, wriggling in the sun, those of them that are motile, and then going on their way. The sense of isolation, peace, elevation is magnificent, and overcome with intentness, I bend further to the task, peering now for the remains of the Flat. They should, as I recall, be emerging quite shortly; the circumstances of the burial were quite disordered and we were not able to do a proper job.

Birds wheel, dart in the air, I work further. The forms however are much closer, a sidelong glance in the act of digging showing me that they are closing ground rapidly and the stick-figures seem to be waving implements of their own, high in the air. Brown and dense they come toward me and now for the first time I can hear their voices. They are shouting. Here they come across the meadow of the infield, the shouts like singing and I dig harder and harder, trying to at least finish the job before the moment of dialogue begins. A bell clangs in the distance, they seem to be readying the starting gate. Dimly I can hear the sound of megaphones, the track announcer seems to be saying something. Since the megaphones are fronted in the opposite direction, I cannot tell what it is but of whatever nature, I am sure that it is most interesting.

Here they come. Ferociously, I continue the digging, meanwhile beginning to talk in a high singing voice, barely able to distinguish the words, listening to myself with the skill and detachment of an auditor. "Oh please," my voice seems to be saying "oh please, oh please," and the Pinkertons, closing the last piece of ground in a rush, vault the rail with splendid precision, ten of them, twenty of them, oh a most significant lot and now I can feel hands, hands on my suit, hands on the pockets, hands tearing the spade from my grasp. "No," I say, fighting them, "no, no, don't stop me," and lean heavily on the shovel, covering it with my body, staggering into a small eave and feeling something horrid under my feet. The spade is torn from my grasp. I hurl myself toward the spade, stumble, fall instead into the depression and collapse with a groan into some object below, feeling bones clatter underneath, feeling something horrid rasp beneath the skin. A Pinkerton leans over to grasp me, loses balance himself and falls atop me and so we lie on the Earth: Harry, myself, the Pinkerton and I am a most uneasy sandwich filler, indeed, kicking and flailing as a new thought occurs to me, something not embraced by my previous calculations. A thought which should have been taken into account but was, of course, not.

"You crazy son of a bitch," someone screams toward me, "you crazy son of a bitch, what the hell do you think you're trying to do? What the hell is on your mind? What the hell are you after?"

I lift my head, then, holding up the Pinkerton with a massive effort, feeling his pressure on me, slipping and sliding beneath as the weaker Harry disintegrates further under our weight. The question is very important and it deserves an answer; I try to phrase things as judiciously as possible so that there will be no chance of being misinterpreted. I could hardly bear, at this late point, to be misunderstood. Clarity of communication is essential; clear linkage in the void. I look at the questioner and lock his eyes and then I speak from the entire heart of me with such force that only the whole world should listen.

"I'm trying to get out," I say.

THE END

My Mission in South Ozone Park

By Barry N. Malzberg

Fifty one years ago, still trying to find a voice and purpose, I wrote a short story "The Ultimate Tip" set at Aqueduct Race Track in South Ozone Park in the Borough of Queens, New York. My hapless protagonist (all of my protagonists then and now are hapless), a horseplayer on a terminal losing streak, is visited by the Devil who offers him the Ultimate Tip, the sure winner in the next day's ninth. The morning line is 50-1, the horse's form is hopeless. A four year old maiden filly named Liz Piet has never finished better than seventh in fifteen races and now, unreasonably, is being stepped up in class. The Devil's bargain is the usual. "High of course but that is the standard deal." My protagonist points out that he has no significant money to wager. "No problem," the Devil says. "I'll lend you a thousand and you can refund that immediately from your winnings." My neo-Faust, sunk in debt and self-destruction, sees no alternative. He takes the deal and leaving his miserable furnished room at dawn, arrives at Aqueduct in early morning, the thousand dollars palpating in his pocket like a tumor. Four hours to post time for the crucial second race.

I will elide agonized synopsis. The Devil is—well, the Devil. His Ultimate Tip has been shared it would seem by everyone at Aqueduct this day. Harry—we might as well call him Harry although he is never to be The Flat— finds himself surrounded, finds himself choked and pressed by the largest crowd he has ever seen at this sprawling, noisome establishment. People surge, chatter, whisper, run. Harry hears them murmur, "Liz Liz Liz Liz." The sibilant steams his consciousness, penetrates him like knives. Suddenly everyone is running to the windows. He finds himself carried as if by a tornado. Six minutes to post time, now five, then four. The lines at the mutual windows are enormous. It is clear that he will be shut out. Thousands are going to be shut out. This is the largest crowd in the history of racing. "Liz," they cry. "Piet Piet Piet." Pitter-pitter-patter. Harry gets a glimpse of the tote board in odd, splintered flashes of light. Liz, the four horse, is 1-5. No, she is 1-9. The board can cast no lower odds. If Harry gets to the window, if he makes his bet, he will win one hundred dollars. And lose his immortal soul. The devil has been busy all night, walking up and down the Earth and to and fro upon it. Caught in the endless, teeming, stunned masses, Harry has an epiphany. It is an old one, of course.

The story was rejected by the *Magazine of Fantasy & Science Fiction*. I am not sure that it was ever sent elsewhere. I had other concerns in the Summer of 1963, not all of them disconnected from the writing of fiction, but I knew that this story was no good. Stark, somewhat clumsy, and the pari-mutuel system made a poor villain, even for readers of fantasy and science fiction. I put it away. I got married. I procured a Shubert Playwriting Fellowship at Syracuse University, embarked upon a convoluted and difficult journey. (It is all in "Tripping With The Alchemist," a long essay in the 6/03 issue of that very *Magazine of Fantasy & Science Fiction*.) Many events, eventual publication, a daughter, Stephanie. Science Fiction. A larger West Side apartment malevolently limned in *Herovit's World*. But the short story stayed with me.

It haunted me: the wretched Liz Piet, the treacherous Devil, the surging, shouting, desperate crowds carrying Harry helplessly toward a destiny suddenly not obscure. Glow of the tote, screams of the trainers, rushing in the paddock, the anguished aspirant straining of the cheap claiming horses, most of them able to race only through illegal pain killers. The glint of fading Winter sun in the shabby light of the tote. And the terror, the madness in the grandstand as tens of thousands came alive slowly to full realization of their betrayal.

I wrote a novel, *Overlay*, in a few weeks in February of 1970 and sold it to Lancer Books. It was fair but Harry was missing as was the Devil and the screams of the betrayed horses. Now it was July and my wife was seven months pregnant and "The Ultimate Tip" was still there, hammering, hammering. *Overlay* had not purged that damned story. I wanted to try again. This time I wanted to write the World Novel which like the World Snake would consume itself: a novel which would sweep from Runyon to Nabokov, to Westlake, from Evan Connell to Mailer to Marcel fucking Proust. I wanted the grandstand and the Devil and Liz, I wanted the surge and the broken, splintered life, I wanted the light and darkness. I wanted the world as gigantic tote, I wanted Harry as Harry the Flat as God himself. I wanted a prose high and low and up and down. I got *Underlay*. I started it in August 1970. It went at a pace even crazier than that of *Overlay*. On page 230 or thereabouts, my father called. My mother was in the hospital, her gall bladder was being removed as we spoke. "Terrible," I agreed. "I hope everything turns out all right." I went back to the novel. Writers can be monsters. Writers, as Janet Malcolm observed, are always selling someone out (usually themselves, she did not add). *Underlay* was done a week before Erika Cornell arrived. I mailed it to George Ernsberger and got drunk (I did that daily in those days, had nothing to do with Erika and only a little to do with Erika.) Erika made her debut on 9/16 and the next day, under some pressure, the delivery check arrived. (The other half of $2500 to keep the record clear.)

George Ernsberger knew as did I that the novel was good but we had little company. Esther Yntema at the Atlantic Monthly Press, that big tease, wrote "the novel should be either longer or shorter." Avon, in the wake of Ernsberger's departure in early 1971, held the novel for the fully allowable four years by contract, publishing it only with the greatest reluctance and in a throwaway paperback original package guaranteeing its obscurity. The only review it received in its first 40 years was from Roger Sale in a *Hudson Review* "fiction roundup" in 1975. Not too bad, Sale wrote. Literary sophistication and technical facility had now so penetrated the culture of would-be or actual writers that even Malzberg, "an ordinary paperback hack," showed some real literary sophistication. The novel had at least one fan who persuaded a small press to attempt a second edition in 1986. It then entered upon an even longer period of obscurity, emerging for an audio edition last year and now, through the grace of Greg Shepard, this new edition.

I still, no less than Harry the Flat and his progenitor, believe in exterior force, divine possibility. I believe in this novel. "I am the medium through which Sacre passed," Stravinsky said of his *Rite of Spring,* and so when I engage in this praise it is not self-praise, I did not write this novel, I merely facilitated its birth the way that Doctors Blumenthal and Bitterman facilitated the debut of Erika Cornell. I believe in the damned book, I believe that in that dour summer of 1970 the Fat Kid in the back room got it together as he never had and never would again. Like the hapless author of *They Shoot Horses, Don't They,* like the wretched Horace McCoy himself I believe that this novel will carry me forward into eternity but only if I accept Harry's deal...I have to be dead to win. No account. Like Liz Piet, my race is run.

Here it is: my dearest, my battered child. I have two daughters. *Underlay* is my son. I sent him once again onto the seas in this frail raft. Be kind to me as the world was not kind to Harry. November will fall in slanted light and America's broken son hears yet again the cries of Dealey Plaza.

—January 2015: New Jersey

Barry N. Malzberg Bibliography

FICTION

In My Parents' Bedroom (1971)
The Falling Astronauts (1971)
Overlay (1972)
Revelations (1972)
Herovit's World (1973)
In the Enclosure (1973)
The Men Inside (1973)
Phase IV (1973; novelization based
  on a story & screenplay by Mayo
  Simon)
Beyond Apollo (1974)
The Destruction of the Temple
  (1974)
Guernica Night (1974)
On a Planet Alien (1974)
Out from Ganymede (1974;
  stories)
The Sodom and Gomorrah
  Business (1974)
The Best of Barry N. Malzberg
  (1975; stories)
Galaxies (1975)
The Gamesman (1975)
Down Here in the Dream Quarter
  (1976; stories)
Scop (1976)
The Last Transaction (1977)
Chorale (1978)
Malzberg at Large (1979; stories)
The Man Who Loved the
  Midnight Lady (1980; stories)
The Cross of Fire (1982)
The Remaking of Sigmund Freud
  (1985)
In the Stone House (2000; stories)
Shiva and Other Stories (2001;
  stories)

The Passage of the Light: The
  Recursive Science Fiction of
  Barry N. Malzberg (2004; ed. by
  Tony Lewis & Mike Resnick;
  stories)
The Very Best of Barry N.
  Malzberg (2013; stories)

As Barry Malzberg

Oracle of the Thousand Hands
  (1968)
Screen (1968)
Bed of Money (1970)
Confessions of Westchester County
  (1970)
The Spread (1971)
Everything Happened to Susan
  (1972)
The Masochist (1972)
Horizontal Woman (1972;
  reprinted as The Social Worker,
  1973)
The Day of the Burning (1974)
The Tactics of Conquest (1974)
Underlay (1974)
The Many Worlds of Barry
  Malzberg (1975; stories)

With Bill Pronzini

Acts of Mercy (1977)
Prose Bowl (1980)
Night Screams (1981)
The Running of the Beasts (1988)
Problems Solved (2003; stories)

As Mike Barry

Lone Wolf series:
Night Raider (1973)
Bay Prowler (1973)
Boston Avenger (1973)
Desert Stalker (1974)
Havana Hit (1974)
Chicago Slaughter (1974)
Peruvian Nightmare (1974)
Los Angeles Holocaust (1974)
Miami Marauder (1974)
Harlem Showdown (1975)
Detroit Massacre (1975)
Phoenix Inferno (1975)
The Killing Run (1975)
Philadelphia Blow-Up (1975)

As Francine di Natale

The Circle (1969)

As Claudine Dumas

The Confessions of a Parisian
  Chambermaid (1969)

As Mel Johnson/M. L. Johnson

Love Doll (1967)
I, Lesbian (1968)
Just Ask (1968; with Playgirl by
  Lou Craig)
Instant Sex (1968)
Chained (1968; with Master of
  Women by March Hastings &
  Love Captive by Dallas Mayo)
Kiss and Run (1968)
Nympho Nurse (1969)
The Sadist (1969)

The Box (1969)
Do It To Me (1969)
Born to Give (1969)
Campus Doll (1969; with High
  School Stud by Robert Hadley)
A Way With All Maidens (1969)

As Howard Lee

Kung Fu #1: The Way of the Tiger,
  the Sign of the Dragon

As Lee W. Mason

Lady of a Thousand Sorrows
  (1977)

As K. M. O'Donnell

Empty People (1969)
The Final War and Other Fantasies
  (1969; stories)
Dwellers of the Deep (1970)
Gather at the Hall of the Planets
  (1971)
In the Pocket and Other S-F Stories
  (1971; stories)
Universe Day (1971; stories)

Elliot B. Reston

The Womanizer (1972)

As Gerrold Watkins

Art of the Fugue (1970)
A Bed of Money (1970)
Giving It Away (1970)
A Satyr's Romance (1970)
Southern Comfort (1972)

NON-FICTION/ESSAYS

The Engines of the Night: Science
Fiction in the Eighties (1982;
essays)
Breakfast in the Ruins (2007;
essays: expansion of Engines of
the Night)
The Business of Science Fiction:
Two Insiders Discuss Writing
and Publishing (2010; with Mike
Resnick)

EDITED ANTHOLOGIES

Final Stage (1974; with Edward L.
Ferman)
Arena (1976; with Edward L.
Ferman)
Graven Images (1977; with Edward
L. Ferman)
Dark Sins, Dark Dreams (1978;
with Bill Pronzini)
The End of Summer: SF in the
Fifties (1979; with Bill Pronzini)

Shared Tomorrows: Science Fiction
in Collaboration (1979; with Bill
Pronzini)
Neglected Visions (1979; with
Martin H. Greenberg & Joseph
D. Olander)
Bug-Eyed Monsters (1980; with
Bill Pronzini)
The Science Fiction of Mark
Clifton (1980; with Martin H.
Greenberg)
The Arbor House Treasury of
Horror & the Supernatural (1981;
with Bill Pronzini & Martin H.
Greenberg)
The Science Fiction of Kris Neville
(1984; with Martin H.
Greenberg)
Uncollected Stars (1986; with Piers
Anthony, Martin H. Greenberg
& Charles G. Waugh)
The Best Time Travel Stories of All
Time (2003)

Other Stark House books you may enjoy...

Clifton Adams Death's Sweet Song /
Whom Gods Destroy $19.95
Benjamin Appel Brain Guy / Plunder $19.95
Benjamin Appel Sweet Money Girl /
Life and Death of a Tough Guy $21.95
Malcolm Braly Shake Him Till He Rattles /
It's Cold Out There $19.95
Gil Brewer Wild to Possess / A Taste for Sin $19.95
Gil Brewer A Devil for O'Shaugnessy /
The Three-Way Split $14.95
Gil Brewer Nude on Thin Ice /
Memory of Passion $19.95
W. R. Burnett It's Always Four O'Clock /
Iron Man $19.95
W. R. Burnett Little Men, Big World /
Vanity Row $19.95
Catherine Butzen Thief of Midnight $15.95
James Hadley Chase Come Easy—Go Easy /
In a Vain Shadow $19.95
Andrew Coburn Spouses & Other Crimes $15.95
Jada M. Davis One for Hell $19.95
Jada M. Davis Midnight Road $19.95
Bruce Elliott One is a Lonely Number /
Elliott Chaze Black Wings Has My Angel $19.95
Don Elliott/Robert Silverberg
Gang Girl / Sex Bum $19.95
Don Elliott/Robert Silverberg
Lust Queen / Lust Victim $19.95
Feldman & Gartenberg (ed)
The Beat Generation & the Angry Young Men $19.95
A. S. Fleischman Look Behind You, Lady /
The Venetian Blonde $19.95
A. S. Fleischman Danger in Paradise /
Malay Woman $19.95
A. S. Fleischman The Sun Worshippers /
Yellowleg $19.95
Ed Gorman The Autumn Dead /
The Night Remembers $19.95
Arnold Hano So I'm a Heel / Flint /
The Big Out $23.95
Orrie Hitt The Cheaters / Dial "M" for Man $19.95
Elisabeth Sanxay Holding Lady Killer /
Miasma $19.95
Elisabeth Sanxay Holding The Death Wish /
Net of Cobwebs $19.95
Elisabeth Sanxay Holding Strange Crime in Bermuda /
Too Many Bottles $19.95
Elisabeth Sanxay Holding The Old Battle-Ax /
Dark Power $19.95
Elisabeth Sanxay Holding The Unfinished Crime /
The Girl Who Had to Die $19.95
Elisabeth Sanxay Holding Speak of the Devil /
The Obstinate Murderer $19.95
Russell James Underground / Collected Stories $14.95
Day Keene Framed in Guilt / My Flesh is Sweet $19.95
Day Keene Dead Dolls Don't Talk / Hunt the Killer /
Too Hot to Hold $23.95

Mercedes Lambert Dogtown / Soultown $14.95
Dan J. Marlowe/Fletcher Flora/Charles Runyon
Trio of Gold Medals $15.95
Dan J. Marlowe The Name of the Game is Death /
One Endless Hour $19.95
Stephen Marlowe Violence is My Business /
Turn Left for Murder $19.95
McCarthy & Gorman (ed) Invasion of the
Body Snatchers: A Tribute $19.95
Wade Miller The Killer / Devil on Two Sticks $19.95
Wade Miller Kitten With a Whip /
Kiss Her Goodbye $19.95
Rick Ollerman Turnabout / Shallow Secrets $19.95
Vin Packer Something in the Shadows /
Intimate Victims $19.95
Vin Packer The Damnation of Adam Blessing /
Alone at Night $19.95
Vin Packer Whisper His Sin /
The Evil Friendship $19.95
Richard Powell A Shot in the Dark /
Shell Game $14.95
Bill Pronzini Snowbound / Games $14.95
Peter Rabe The Box / Journey Into Terror $19.95
Peter Rabe Murder Me for Nickels /
Benny Muscles In $19.95
Peter Rabe Blood on the Desert /
A House in Naples $19.95
Peter Rabe My Lovely Executioner /
Agreement to Kill $19.95
Peter Rabe Anatomy of a Killer /
A Shroud for Jesso $14.95
Peter Rabe The Silent Wall /
The Return of Marvin Palaver $19.95
Peter Rabe Kill the Boss Good-By /
Mission for Vengeance $19.95
Peter Rabe Dig My Grave Deep / The Out is Death /
It's My Funeral $21.95
Brian Ritt Paperback Confidential:
Crime Writers $19.95
Sax Rohmer Bat Wing / Fire-Tongue $19.95
Douglas Sanderson Pure Sweet Hell /
Catch a Fallen Starlet $19.95
Douglas Sanderson The Deadly Dames /
A Dum-Dum for the President $19.95
Charlie Stella Johnny Porno $15.95
Charlie Stella Rough Riders $15.95
John Trinian North Beach Girl /
Scandal on the Sand $19.95
Harry Whittington A Night for Screaming /
Any Woman He Wanted $19.95
Harry Whittington To Find Cora /
Like Mink Like Murder / Body and Passion $23.95
Harry Whittington Rapture Alley / Winter Girl /
Strictly for the Boys $23.95
Charles Williams Nothing in Her Way /
River Girl $19.95

Stark House Press, 1315 H Street, Eureka, CA 95501
707-498-3135   www.StarkHousePress.com

Retail customers: freight-free, payment accepted by check or paypal via website. Wholesale: 40%, freight-free on
10 mixed copies or more, returns accepted. All books available direct from publisher or Baker & Taylor Books.

Made in the USA
San Bernardino, CA
27 March 2015